{kyra's story}

degrees OF GUILT

Each one plays a part . . .

kyra's story
{DANDI DALEY MACKALL}

miranda's story
{MELODY CARLSON}

tyrone's story
{SIGMUND BROUWER}

{kyra's story}

degrees OF GUILT

DANDI DALEY MACKALL

thirsty™

Tyndale House Publishers, Inc.
Wheaton, Illinois

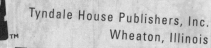

Library of Congress Cataloging-in-Publication Data

Mackall, Dandi Daley.
   Kyra's story / Dandi Daley Mackall.
     p. cm. — (Degrees of guilt series)
Summary: When seventeen-year-old Kyra of Macon, Iowa, becomes overwhelmed by
the stress of senior year in high school, the school play, and early admission to drama
school she begins taking prescription drugs, unaware that her twin brother will suffer
the consequences.
   ISBN 0-8423-8284-4 (sc)
   [1. Drug abuse—Fiction. 2. Brothers and sisters—Fiction. 3. High schools—Fiction.
4. Schools—Fiction. 5. Conduct of life—Fiction. 6. Iowa—Ficiton.] I. Title. II. Series.
PZ7.M1905 Ky 2003
[Fic]—dc21   2003008782

Printed in the United States of America

07   06   05   04   03
7   5   4   3   2

To Karen Watson—Thanks for your
vision and heart for this project

To Ramona Cramer Tucker—Thanks for
your boundless energy and spirit
and your amazing edits

I'd like to thank a number of people
who helped me in my research:
Judge Vercillo of Ashland County;
Tom Getz, Cleveland attorney;
my own kids—Jen, Dan, and Katy—and their friends;
my husband, Joe, who is always my greatest help.
Thanks to the Tyndale team and the Web crew,
who get as excited about the books as I do.
And thanks to the other authors of our trilogy,
Melody Carlson and Sigmund Brouwer.

They killed Sammy. Maybe we all did.

He's dead. He died.

Don't you dare—not any of you—try saying my brother is *gone*, that he *passed, passed away, passed over*, had a terrible *accident*.

Sammy was 17. Now he's dead. Just like that.

Dylan says Sammy is in heaven. But even that doesn't make him less dead . . . or us less guilty.

I'm sitting on a shiny wooden bench outside the courtroom. Footsteps echo through the hall—people in a hurry, with places to go, people to go to. A door slams somewhere, and a burst of voices tangles and bounces against the cold cement walls.

Above, to my right, a branch scrapes a high window. Rain blurs the windowpane—blown there hard, smacked to a stop and dropped, sliding down in sheets, like hands grasping but finding nothing to hold.

"I'm afraid it's going to be a while, Kyra." The D.A. smiles at me like she's afraid I'll change my mind about testifying. She sets down her briefcase and gives me a we're-in-this-together nod. Just two girls here. But Sammy wasn't *her* twin. And she should know *she'd* back down before I would.

"I'm okay," I say.

"It's good to go over your testimony in your head if you want to, while you're waiting." She tugs at her thin black ponytail and unbuttons her gray suit jacket. "Remember, just answer the questions. You're going to do fine, Kyra." She picks up her briefcase and goes back into the courtroom.

I try to see inside, but only get a glimpse of the guard at the door and part of a row of strangers in the back.

I've watched enough bad TV and *Law and Order* reruns to know you can't always trust judges and juries. They can't always trust the witnesses sworn in to tell the truth, the whole truth, and nothing but the truth. People shape their stories, their *truth*, to make themselves look better, to make the world a place they can live in without going crazy. I know that better than anybody.

So maybe people won't get what they deserve in this trial. Sammy sure didn't deserve what he got.

I stand up, pace down the hall, and glance both ways through the corridor. No Miranda. No Tyrone. I don't even know for sure if they'll show. I don't have any idea what they're going to say or who will believe them.

Maybe they won't believe me. Maybe nobody will. I can't blame them. For 17 years I didn't believe me either.

But believe *this*. Sammy James is dead. And somebody has to know how it happened, how we really got to this, a murder trial in Macon, Iowa, the first in our town's history.

So I might as well write it all down. I won't leave anything out—I'll tell it just like it happened. It all started New Year's Day, when Mitchell Wade sauntered into town like a New Year's resolution somebody forgot to make, a resolution that, from that moment on, changed life as we knew it.

"No, look! Across the street! Getting into his car?" I pause for effect.

Miranda Sanchez is sitting beside me in the booth. She's the closest to the window and presses her nose below the backward yellow letters spelling out *Tiger Den.* The Den is one of the two places open on New Year's Day in Macon, Iowa.

"Who do you see, Kyra?" Miranda asks, cupping her long fingers around her blue eyes. Her eyes are her least Latino feature. She's a head taller than I am, with long dark hair I'd kill for. She's wearing sweats and a shirt straight from the Helen Keller school of design.

"It's Adam Sandler," I announce, leaning back in the orange booth and folding my arms in front of me.

Across from Miranda and me, Jamal Jackson and D.J. frown out the ice-laced window. Snow has piled in the corners like mini-mountains. D.J.'s the reason we're all here, although I'm the only one who knows it. I decided it's high time for D.J. Johnson to ask Kyra James out. Sammy tipped me off that D.J. and Jamal were chowing down at the Den.

Ten minutes later, so were Miranda and I.

It hasn't taken much to draw the three of them into my personality-spotting game. We have never had a famous person set foot in Macon, so I hunt look-alikes and pretend. Passes the time.

Miranda turns back around in the booth. "Kyra's right, you guys. What's-his-name? Gleason? Guy from auto parts? He's a dead ringer for Adam Sandler."

"No way," D.J. mutters.

He's not articulate, and it comes out *"Nway."* But it doesn't matter. D.J. Johnson is ripped. So ripped, but laid back. Think long legs and bendable, like all his joints and points have been worn down like river rocks, like you knew his mother had to be one of those "D.J., no slumping at the table," "D.J., sit up straight" kind of mothers before she gave up.

"Okay. They look kinda the same," D.J. admits, taking a second look.

"Yeah," Jamal says, dipping a curly fry into ketchup and downing it, "but all you white guys look alike."

I grab two fries and scarf them down like I'm not even noticing.

D.J. notices. I can tell. He takes a fry. I take two.

Research. I've done my homework on D.J. Johnson. He's the only major datable left to conquer in our fair town. In five months we graduate from Macon High. Good thing. I have history with just about every male Maconian. D.J. has three sisters—"good eaters," Gram would have said. I know he's used to seeing girls eat hardy. Picky, girlish eaters would make him uncomfortable.

Exact opposite of Manny, the big football star, who prefers girls to be little more than feminine decoration. When I targeted him, I made sure I never finished anything and never, ever ate fries or desserts.

"Can I have a bite?" I ask, leaning across the table and taking a big bite of D.J.'s burger. Burger with onions, I discover. I'll have to skip dinner *and* breakfast to make up for this.

"How do you eat so much and keep so skinny, girl?" Jamal asks, playing into my hand. "My sister counts every calorie she puts into her mouth."

"I never thought about it," I lie, taking D.J.'s pickle. I raise my eyebrows in a silent plea for it. He nods. "I just eat when I feel like it."

"No fair," says our waitress, as she rips off our bills from her little pad. Laurie's worked at the Tiger Den since before we were born. She's plump, but in a way I think looks good on older people. "Skinny little thing like you?" She plops our separate bills on the table, lining them in a straight, upside-down row. "Anything else?"

"Maybe later?" I smile at her and get a wink.

It makes me think she remembers my other dates here, when I left most of my meal on my plate.

The door opens. An icy gust fans in as the bell over the door rings—like anybody would need announcing in the Macon Tiger Den. Dylan Gray rushes in, pulls off his stocking cap, and waves it at us.

"Hey, Dylan!" I call, motioning him over. No sweat if he joins us. Everybody and their brother know Dylan and I don't date. We've been buddies since before kindergarten. We fought over the same toys in the church nursery. Our families even took vacations together a couple of years in a row. We stopped when Bethany, Dylan's little sister, was born with too many medical problems for the Grays to risk getting far from her doctors.

Miranda scoots over so I can make room for Dylan next to me. "You missed Lucille Ball, Cher, Drew Barrymore, Austin Powers . . . and Tommy Lee Jones," Miranda says.

Dylan does his half-grin, making his dimple. He knows the personality game. I used to make him play it with me. In those days, we spotted Mr. Rogers, Barney, and that *Home Alone* kid. Dylan's hair is long, a day away from the barber, and his glasses are fogged. He's the only guy I know, though, who looks great in glasses, better than without them. He played freshman and sophomore football but dropped out last year to keep up his grades and work in his dad's lumberyard.

Jamal slides the plate of fries to Dylan. "You also missed Adam Sandler."

"Ah . . ." Dylan shakes his head no to fries. "But I'm in time for Gary Peyton." He nods to Jamal, so I figure it's some sports hero. "Ben Affleck." A fair assessment of D.J., only D.J.'s more of a stud. Dylan grins at Miranda. "Sandra Bullock." He turns to me, eyes narrowing. We lock stares, Dylan and I. When we were kids, I used to know what he'd say before he said it. Not anymore.

"Hmmm." He rubs his chin, touches his glasses, and sighs.

I'm ready to kick him if he says I'm somebody D.J. will think is ugly or uncool.

"This is a tough one." Dylan tilts his head for a better look at me. "Blonde, green eyes . . . it's either . . . a thin Marilyn Monroe or Britney Spears with soul. Hard to say."

Not bad. Even Dylan's working for me tonight. "So, Dylan, how was your New Year's Eve? Where did you go again?" I know before he answers that it has something to do with church and the youth group I haven't gone to since junior high. Dylan still invites Sammy and me to things a couple of times a year. Sammy usually goes.

"We had a New Year's Eve party that ended up in the church gym with a great Christian rock group. I think you would have liked them, Kyra."

Come on, Dylan! Ask me what I did.

"What did you end up doing?"

Yes! "Don't ask," I say, taking the last fry. "Horrible date. Only good thing about it is that it was my first, and it'll be my absolutely last date with Tyrone." *Hear that, D.J.?*

"You serious?" Miranda asks.

"Is Barbie thin?" I answer, wishing I'd gone for a basketball analogy. D.J.'s into ball.

Dylan takes a sip of my Coke. It makes me sad. I think I'm remembering when we used to be so close we shared school lunches. Or maybe the weird feeling I'm getting is just my body's way of telling me it doesn't like French fry grease.

"I can't keep up with you, Kyra," Dylan complains.

"I thought you and Tyrone were going out?" Jamal leans back in the booth. His legs stretch to our side and then some.

"Never." I risk a glance at D.J. He's looking at me but shifts his eyes back to his empty plate. "That was our first official date. And nevermore, as the Raven said." *Stupid! Barbie and Poe? I have to read up on basketball quotes.*

"What happened?" Dylan's studying me now, his brown eyes slits behind wire-framed glasses.

I shrug. "Let's not go there, okay?"

I see that D.J.'s finished his burger and is reading the milk-shake flavors written in black marker on the white menu board hung over the counter, like something new could actually appear there.

I nudge Dylan. "Scooch! Lemme outta here! I'm still hungry." Of course, I'm not hungry. But I have to get D.J. by himself. He's not brave enough to ask me out in front of Jamal. Couldn't take the razzing if I turned him down, which I won't. But he doesn't know that.

"D.J.?" I give him my best smile. "C'mon. I'm

thinking milk shake, a new flavor creation . . .
chocolate definitely, with maybe fudge, and possibly peanut butter?"

He gets up. His tennis shoes are so big they catch on the table leg.

I manage to bump into him when I slide out.
"Sorry." I grab his arm to steady myself. Clumsy me.
I don't come up to his shoulder. He's way taller than my brother, and Sammy is six-one barefooted. Jamal and Sammy are the best players on Macon's basketball squad, but D.J.'s not half-bad.

D.J. and I walk to the counter, me still holding his arm. Not holding exactly, just touching.

"So, D.J., did you have a great New Year's Eve, like everybody seems to have had except me?"

He shrugs.

I know he went out with Tressa. We're cheerleading buddies, but all's fair in love, plus I know they didn't have that great of a time. I told you I did my homework.

Laurie the Waitress—who's probably younger than my mom but looks 10 years older because she's a smoker without the benefits of Mom's oils, masks, and ointments—is the only one on duty tonight, except for Mr. Fisher in the back. She's refilling coffee for a man. I should know his name. He drives a truck and has a son who used to be friends with Sammy.

"I wish I'd broken my date with Tyrone and just gone by myself to see that new Vin Diesel movie like I wanted to."

D.J. stops reading the flavors and frowns down

at me as if he's never seen me before. "You like Vin Diesel?"

Bingo.

"Who wouldn't? *The Fast and the Furious? Triple X?* Classics!" I'm hoping he won't ask me about the movies because all I know is what Sammy said after he saw them with Jamal and some other guys. I hate car-chase movies. But they are *so* D.J.

"Vin is tight! I loved *Fast and Furious!*" It's the most he's said since he ordered his meal.

You've hooked him. Easy now. Reel him in easy. "They say that new movie's his best," I claim, thinking the guy's best probably isn't that hot. "It's playing at Clarinda, but I'll bet you anything it only runs through tomorrow night. If I miss it, I'm going to be so bummed."

"Me too." He's thinking. I can almost hear the wheels turning. "Hey, you wanna go see it?"

"Of course," I answer, pretending I don't get his meaning.

"Like with me? Tomorrow before it leaves Clarinda?"

"Tomorrow night?" I repeat. "Sure."

Ta-da. Mission accomplished. Operation D.J., a success!

I order a large chocolate-peanut-butter-fudge milk shake just to be on the safe side. And I get a lid so D.J. won't notice I'm not actually drinking the stuff.

It's all I can do not to strut back to the booth. I want to tell Miranda, but she's arguing with Jamal about something. I hear her say "Sam" and I'm about to ask her what they're talking about when the bell rings and the door opens.

Jamal and Miranda stop arguing. D.J. and I, halfway back to the booth, stop walking. It feels like all the air is sucked out of the Den, vacuum-packing us together.

You wouldn't have to have grown up in Macon to know the guy who just walked in isn't from around here. Nobody here has a long cashmere overcoat like that. Nobody in all of Iowa has a tan like this guy's—rich and golden even though it's the dead of winter. And that hair—brown, thick, brushing his forehead—was not cut in the Macon Unisex and Shears Shop on Main Street.

I've never seen anyone this handsome this close up. He's not high school, but not old. Maybe college. Maybe out a couple of years.

Someone drops a fork, and the clang of it jump-starts the room's heartbeat again. D.J. moves toward the booth. Jamal laughs. Dylan stands up to let me slide back into the booth.

The tanned wonder orders coffee, black, and thanks Laurie in a voice as low and warm as coffee.

Laurie stands there staring at him until he has to ask her how much he owes her. "Fifty cents," Laurie says, even though coffee at the Den has been 55 cents since last Easter.

"Thank you," he says. "It smells perfect."

Nobody in Iowa would say that.

He turns to leave, but he pauses—just a second too long—and glances at our booth, sizing us up, one after the other.

Dylan clears his throat. Miranda bites her nonexistent thumbnail. Jamal brushes crumbs off his lap. Even D.J. sits up straighter.

I stare back. And something happens between us. I feel it inside, deep in the spaces between my bones. And I think he feels it, too. Who is he?

The door shuts. Who was he?

Miranda breaks our awkward silence. "Kevin Costner? No! Harrison Ford in that first *Star Wars* movie."

"I haven't seen *him* around before," Dylan says, leaning in front of me to peer through the window. The night has turned pitch-black, without a single star breaking through. "Man, take a look at those wheels! What is that, Jamal? Porsche 911?"

In the background Mr. Fisher's scratchy radio is playing an old country-western song. I try to hear the lyrics, straining for the words wailed from the kitchen, as if they hold secret meaning, a code woven around ordinary words.

Dylan leaves. Then Jamal. So there's only Miranda, D.J., and me. The slurp of D.J.'s straw is our only contribution to the Den's audio track.

"So what time, Kyra?" D.J. asks.

It's a second before I realize he's talking to me, asking me something. "What?" I look up from where I've twisted my straw cover into a wrinkled ball.

"What time you want I should come pick you up tomorrow?" D.J. asks.

Miranda punches my leg under the table.

I try to focus. D.J. Pick me up. The movie. "Six,"

I say. But I can still smell *him*—something tropical, totally not sold here, a fresh scent filled with promise and mystery. And I think if I don't see him again—the tanned, brown-haired stranger with eyes that bore through me—I think I'll die.

Sunday morning, Mom hollers upstairs, "Sam! Kyra! Last call. We'll be late to church. Pancakes!"

I smell the pancakes, but I won't be eating them. I had buttered popcorn and Milk Duds at the movies with D.J. I stumble toward the bathroom, but Sammy slips by me.

"And the world-famous basketball star fades left, turns . . ." Sammy's way too awake for morning. ". . . shoots and scores!" He shoves into the john and shuts the door.

Too tired to fight, I slip to the floor, my back against the white wall. "Hurry, Sammy! I'm waiting out here."

"How was the movie?" Sammy shouts from the other side of the wooden door.

"Stupid guy flick," I answer truthfully. "D.J. loved it."

Sammy laughs. I hear water running. "What did you two talk about anyway?" The words are garbled through toothpaste.

"Life and love and world peace," I lie. D.J. and I didn't talk, not through the whole dumb movie or on the drive back. True, I managed to keep the verbiage flowing by dropping effective openers like, "What did you think of that last car chase?" But I didn't listen to his answers. I couldn't even tell you what the movie was about.

Most of the time I just looked around the theater, especially during the explosion scenes, when I could see better. I tried to make out each form and face, imagining *him* all over again, the tanned stranger from the Tiger Den. I'd even made D.J. drive once around the parking lot when we got there, under the pretext that we could find a better spot. I was scoping for the Porsche.

D.J. looked cute as ever, all cleaned up and smelling like Brut. And the guy cleans up nice. But I couldn't stop thinking about the stranger. He had stopped in Macon, Iowa, and bought coffee. And Macon is not exactly on the way to anywhere.

He was still in town. I knew it. I could sense his presence.

Sammy emerges from the bathroom, shirtless and smiling. "Blueberry pancakes." He really can eat all he wants and never get fat. I hate him.

I haul myself to my feet. "Where'd you disappear to last night, little brother?" I ask, remembering that he wasn't in his room when I got in at midnight. Sammy is almost three minutes younger than I am, and I've gotten big-time mileage out of that fact, mileage I need since he now has me by over half a foot and 80 pounds easy.

Sammy turns his enigmatic winsome smile on me, which works on our mother 100 percent of the time. "I was skipping the light fantastic."

He takes the stairs down in three leaps, and I hear him explode into the kitchen. "My mother is the best cook in the U.S. of A.!"

I hear *our* mother laugh.

■   ■   ■

Half an hour later we're sitting in Dad's Buick, waiting for Sammy. Dad's already backed out of the garage, but he refuses to turn on the heater until we're off our street and the engine is warm. It's freezing and gray out, barely light because of the clouds hovering.

"Let's leave him," I suggest, only half-joking. I don't enjoy church and just want to get it over with. I don't hate it or anything. Pastor Jim is even pretty good, sorta funny sometimes. I just don't like the white gospel music the choir hangs on to. Plus, there are a lot of ways I could use Sunday mornings if I didn't have to be in church. But Mom and Dad insist.

Dad honks the horn. The nose of the car is still close enough to the garage for the beep to echo off walls. Rakes and yard brooms hang on one wall, sports equipment is in neat rows on the opposite wall, and gardening supplies are shelved on the third. "We're not rich," Dad loves to say, "but we take care of what we have."

Nobody in Macon, Iowa, is rich. I know some of my friends, like Miranda, think we are. Both of my parents work—Dad for an ad agency in Clarinda and Mom at one of the two Macon real-estate offices. Her specialty is big office complexes and corporate space. Just once I'd like to see her in action with big businessmen. At home she's no match for Dad, and she doesn't seem to want to be.

I lean over the front seat and honk the horn myself.

Sammy strolls out, shrugging into his coat as he walks to the car. He has to fold himself into the backseat. "Sorry," he says, shutting the door.

"I've known glaciers that move faster," I mutter.

He leans over and whispers to me, "But were they this cool? Takes time for *cool*." He dramatically finger-combs his brown hair.

I glare at him. I'm supposed to be the funny one. Sammy is so *not* a primper anyway. Not considered *cool* either.

Dad backs down the drive and signals to pull onto our street, even though no cars are in sight.

"Kyra, I almost forgot." Mom's been checking her lipstick in the mirror. We do eye contact in the tiny rectangular glass on the visor. She's pulled her auburn hair back into a jeweled barrette. I can see cobwebbed lines at the corners of her eyes and wonder how long it will be before I have them too.

I dated a guy once who said all a man had to do to know what his future wife would be like in 20 years was to look at the girl's mother now.

"That woman from NYU called," Mom continues, using her pinkie to smooth out her eyebrows. "They're sending you the new forms to fill out for summer school. And they're looking forward to our visit next week and introducing you to some of the theater people."

I nod at the mirror. "Thanks." I try to remember the moment we decided I'd go to New York University and major in theater, but I can't. I can't even remember a time when I didn't know that's where I'd end up. It doesn't really matter.

Dad chimes in. "That summer course at NYU should put you way ahead of the game, Kyra. You can get to know the profs, and they'll get to know you. Smaller group, first impressions—all good. We'll come up for the production at the end of the summer, meet your teachers."

My stomach plunges to the pit of my belly and gnarls there. Maybe it's because I skipped breakfast.

"I'll bet your resumé is stronger than any of the other freshmen." Dad seems to be talking to himself.

None of us interrupts.

When Sammy and I were maybe one or two, we still looked a lot alike for fraternal twins—big eyes, chubby, blond curls, which Dad eventually made Mom cut off the "son." A client of Dad's saw our photo on Dad's desk in his office and talked him into using us for his ad campaign. Dad didn't take much convincing.

The product was "Children's Ice"—teething rings. Those cold plastic circles parents give kids when they're cutting new teeth so they don't cry so much. The slogan was, "Take two and you won't have to call anyone in the morning." I guess it was a big hit, and so were Sammy and I.

After that, we did two more commercials, one for baby food and one for milk. The milk ad ran all year on national TV. I even had a speaking line: "Milk mine!"

But Sammy had a growth spurt and ended our twin acting career. By the time we were four, you couldn't even tell we were twins.

"What's the play going to be this year?" Dad asks, turning the corner, blinker clicking. Our church comes into view, and the lot is nearly full. "Neil Carter at the office says his son Tony's trying out just for the chance of being onstage with you. When you're famous, he wants to be able to say he played onstage with Kyra James." Dad laughs, but he means it.

"Mrs. Overstreet said it's Shakespeare, but I'm not sure if she decided on *Taming of the Shrew* or *As You Like It.*"

"That's perfect, honey!" Mom exclaims, brushing something off her blue church dress and rebuttoning one of the buttons.

"Especially if it's *Taming of the Shrew*," Sammy adds. "Typecasting."

I elbow him. But I feel like I might hurl, and I'm dying to get out of the car now.

I've had the lead in every play since the kindergarten program, when by all accounts, I stole the show as Mrs. Santa Claus and covered for my poor husband, who forgot his lines as soon as we stepped in front of the audience.

Mrs. Overstreet went through the motions of tryouts for all parts in our freshman production, although she and I had talked about the play as if I had the lead. After that, she just asked our class if anybody minded if she gave me the title role. Last year I was *The Unsinkable Molly Brown*. Nobody minded. Especially when more people bought tickets to our junior play than to the big senior production of *Once upon a Mattress*.

The front parking lot is full, but Dad creates his own parking spot in front of the vending machine.

We make our way at different speeds through people in the foyer. Our pew is third from the back, on the middle aisle. Sammy's still talking with Shawna and her friend, Alyssa, who couldn't flirt harder if she flashed him.

The organ music starts, and Sammy dashes over and scoots next to me in our pew. He always sits on my left. He used to do it so I could whisper to him during church and have his good ear handy. When we were 10, he was cleaning his left ear with a Q-Tip. I bumped his elbow for a joke, and the Q-Tip went into his eardrum and messed up his hearing in his left ear. It was our first trip to the emergency room. Even after surgery, he never got all of his hearing back, although most people never notice.

"Flirting in church will get you a ticket down under, Sammy," I whisper.

Sammy has turned in the pew, so my whisper ends up more in the bad ear than the good. "Huh?"

I think better of it. "Nothing. I like the Bach." The one good thing about Sammy's bad ear is that lots of times I get a second chance to say something nicer. Dylan and I used to call Sammy the "King of Second Chances." Dylan said he wondered what the world would be like if nobody heard anybody the first time and we all got a second chance to say something better.

"I hate this dress," Mom mutters, buttoning two white pearls that have popped unbuttoned in her lap. The dress is too small for her and has been for over a year. She's not fat, just thicker everywhere, especially at the hips. But we don't admit this.

"You look fine, Linda," Dad says, his gaze moving systematically down the right third of the sanctuary.

I do the same thing, scan the crowd. Only I think I'm expecting to see the tanned stranger here. I don't know what Dad's hoping to see.

"Are you sure?" Mom tugs the hem over her knees.

"You look great," Dad says.

I think she does look pretty good for 45. But she *is* 45. At least Mom stopped smoking before she got leathery like Cindy, her friend from work.

Not that Mom ever admitted smoking or quitting smoking. She was a bathroom smoker. I have never seen my mother so much as hold a cigarette, much less smoke one. But I used to think smoke was a part of the bathroom environment. When I opened the bathroom door after Mom left, I never knew if I'd be greeted with waves of gray smoke and a weird, stale smell.

When I was in junior high, Dad started bringing home nicotine gum and the patch. I don't think he and Mom had discussed it or ever mentioned Mom's smoking habit head-on. Instead Dad left his kick-the-habit props on Mom's dresser or in her purse. One of them must have worked because the bathroom stopped smoking. Either that, or Mom found a foolproof method of hiding her habit.

"Kyra!" The call rises over Bach and is followed by a *shush*. Bethany Gray is kneeling in her pew, turned backwards to face me through the five intervening rows of people. She waves, and her silky, green sleeve slides down her arm. I can see her big brother's hand stuck automatically behind her waist, ready to catch her if she slips.

I wave to Bethany, and she waves back twice as hard. I'm not sure I believe in angels. But if they exist, I think they all look like Bethany—round face, tiny blue eyes that send out light from inside, and a smile that's so total, so pure and out there, that you wish you could bottle it. She's small for her age, looks more like seven than nine, with tiny fingers and stiff arms.

Bethany was diagnosed with Down's syndrome at birth. The doctors warned the Grays ahead of time and gave them "options." The Grays were already pretty religious—we all were in a way, I guess. But Bethany was insurance that the Gray family would keep in touch with God.

The day she was born, even though you could tell she was different just by looking at her face, which looked like pictures of other kids with Down's syndrome, you never saw two happier people than Bethany's parents. Make that three, counting Dylan.

I pull three green-and-white peppermints from my purse, slide the long way out of our pew because I only have to climb over Sammy, and slip down the aisle to Bethany.

She takes the mints and hugs my neck. "Thank you, Kyra."

Mrs. Gray grins up at me.

Dylan holds out his hand.

"Sorry, guy," I say, palms up.

Bethany instantly gives Dylan two mints, which he returns to her with a scruff of her thin, blonde hair.

I tiptoe back to my seat as the choir starts its first song about being lost.

I know I should pay attention to the sermon, but I keep thinking about school starting again, my last semester. I'm wondering if Tyrone Larson's theory is right—that we could ditch every remaining day of class and it wouldn't matter.

I'm already accepted at NYU. But I'm feeling the same anxiety I've felt every day before school since kindergarten. Even then I worried about the teacher not liking me, the other kids making fun of me. It didn't happen. In fact, I'd been shocked that Sammy and I were the only ones who already knew all our capital and small letters. I pretended not to know the *U*s from the *W*s so kids wouldn't think I was *too* smart.

I let the pastor's words drift in the high-arched ceiling, while I scan the backs of heads in my line of vision. Amazing how many men are bald or balding. Maybe that's what my dad was eyeing the crowd for. He has a full head of black wavy hair. My friends think he's handsome, but you can't tell by me.

I imagine the tanned stranger sitting somewhere behind me and to the side, watching me, his gaze boring into my skull as he wonders who I am and whether or not I noticed him New Year's Day. I sit straighter, smooth my hair, and turn my head just enough to give my best profile.

Then it's over.

Dad makes us all go out to eat in Clarinda. I get by ordering a salad, no dressing, and nibbling the lettuce until they're finished.

■   ■   ■

The phone rings as soon as we step into the house. Mom picks it up. "Hello?"

I'm on the second step, heading upstairs, but I can tell by Mom's phone voice it's a guy, probably for me. She covers the receiver with her palm. "Kyra, for you!"

"Who is it?" I ask.

"P.J. Something?"

She means D.J., and I don't feel like rehashing Vin Diesel's career. I don't know if I want to go out

with D.J. again or not. "Tell him I'm not here!"
I call down.

Mom hollers, "Kyra?" She's against lies of the
bald-faced variety.

"Tell him I have a headache." It's the excuse
I gave Dad in the restaurant when he wanted me
to eat a roll. As soon as I say it, I realize it's true
now. I really do have a headache.

I trot on upstairs. Mom will handle D.J. better
than I could right now. She never wants to discour-
age any of them. If she only knew. . . .

I'm not sure what's wrong with me, why I don't
feel like talking to D.J. or to anybody, why I don't
want to think about school tomorrow, but then I *do*
want to think about it.

Sammy's changed into sweats already and is
headed back down the stairs, basketball in hand.

I block his path near the top of the stairs.
"Sammy, do you still have your econ book from
last semester?" I've put off economics as long as
possible. Mr. Hatt will be the only teacher I haven't
taken before. I want to make a good impression
and get that over with. It would help if I could
glance through the text before class.

"Yeah, right." Sammy bounces the ball on the
stairs and then folds his long arms around it. "My
beloved econ book is right beside my bed with my
algebra book, framed." He fakes left and twirls past
me on the right.

My muscles jerk in the pit of my stomach. I'm
so tired of worrying about everything . . . and
nothing. I don't want to think anymore, not about

econ or school or D.J. or Vin Diesel. Not about anything.

I open the door to my room and wonder why it doesn't feel more like home, like *my* room. I got to choose new wallpaper last year, but I went with the one I could tell Mom was rooting for— sky blue with slightly raised white puffs through it. It looks fine. I wouldn't have known what else to pick.

The desk is built in like a long counter with drawers on both sides. I never study there though. I sit on the floor or on my bed. The only poster, tack-mounted on my closet door, is the one Miranda gave me during her Beatles phase. John Lennon, looking so sad you could almost believe he knew what was coming.

I don't collect things like most of my friends. So the glass figurines on my wall shelf are things people have given me.

The CD tower by my bed is full, mostly with CDs guys have liked and given me or burned copies for me. When I dated Drew, I pretended to like the rap he ran through his car speakers, so he burned me about 20 rap CDs. Same with Dan, only he was into heavy metal.

I take the bottom CD without looking at it and stick it in my portable player. Then I plop onto my bed and lean back, facing the white, stucco ceiling.

I crank up the volume all the way before I put on the headphones. I like the surprise, the shock of sound when I slip on the headset. It's loud—

head-shaking, teeth-jarring loud—like I've stepped inside a tunnel where I can't escape, but neither can the music.

"So? Tell me everything!" Tressa demands. "And great sweater, by the way."

We're sitting in the back row in Mrs. Overstreet's classroom, first-period English Lit. I ducked in early to avoid D.J., who hasn't signed on for an English course since he met core requirements. Tressa's followed me into the room to pump me about my date with D.J. At least she's not acting angry.

I shrug.

"Give!" She's wearing jeans, too, with a green tank and olive button-down sweater. Her red hair is pulled back in a gold clip. "I told *you* about *my* D.J. date."

"No big deal, Tressa, okay? He was . . . he was just D.J. And the movie was so testosterone."

Kids are trickling in. First bell rings. Tressa and

I nod and wave when we should to kids we should. Almost everybody's wearing something new—a shirt, sweater, shoes, purse.

"Did he put the moves on you?" she asks, shouldering me.

"Hello? He *is* D.J. I handled him."

Tressa knows too much about my dating life already. I never learned the facts of life from Jeff and Linda James. It would have been too embarrassing for all of us. When I was 13, Mom brought home two pamphlets from the clinic's waiting room—"Your Body and You" (I'm not kidding) and "Now That You're Becoming a Woman."

Miranda and I read them for laughs at lunch one Tuesday in the school cafeteria.

I learned the "facts" from Dylan—what he knew at age nine, all very scientific and stopping way short of embarrassing me, although *his* face turned red when he said the word *puberty*. Most of the rest was filled in by Tressa a couple of years later. That kid knew what was what before we left elementary school.

What remained of the mystery, Danny Galavetto had tried to demonstrate for me my ninth-grade year in the back of his dad's Volvo. Thank heavens for Dylan and Tressa, who had gone before him. I knew where to draw the lines.

Tressa wants more. "So did he tell you he—?"

Miranda walks in, looking like she thinks she's taken the wrong school bus.

"Miranda!" I shout. "Back here!"

She slides between the rows of chairs to get to

the back. She's wearing a new sweater, probably
a Christmas present from her mom, probably pur-
chased when her mom was high. Big yellow flowers
bloom all over the black short sweater. Still, I watch
guys watch her move. Guys who say hi to her are
rewarded with a furtive, Julia-Roberts smile. Her
dark hair waves carelessly to her shoulders.

"Have I ever told you I hate school?" Miranda
asks, flinging her pack to the floor and plopping
into the chair next to me. She crosses her legs at the
ankles. She's wearing black wool socks and granny
boots. I like the boots. "But it doesn't matter. This
semester I'm all about fun."

"Sure you are, Miranda," I say. She may not get
as uptight as I do about school, but *she* shows her
nerves. I think if I had her home and her whacked-
out mother, I'd be the first one in line when they
opened the school doors after break.

"Sammy tell you we made a snowman last
night?" Miranda asks, taking a pen out of her pack
and tapping it on the desk arm of her chair. "Right
on Coach's front lawn! Not a bad representation,
if I do say so myself."

"Sammy tells me nothing." I straighten her collar,
tucking in the tiny tag at the back. "He better hope
Coach didn't see him do it though."

The room has grown noisy with guys shouting
across desks at each other. Sammy and Jamal are
sitting close to the door, locked in arm wrestling
and surrounded by cheering spectators, most of
them rooting for my brother.

Five more minutes pass. In all three of my English

classes with Mrs. Overstreet, she made it a point to get there early. She's never once been this late.

"I say we walk if Mrs. O. isn't here in five," Tyrone mutters.

"The woman is late. Give her a break," I say. I'm never sure why, but when I say something, anything, people get quiet. Makes me wish I had more to say. "Punctuality is the thief of time!" I proclaim, enunciating each word dramatically. "Oscar—"

"Wilde." Someone's finished my quotation. We all turn to the doorway to see who.

It's him.

I realize my mouth is open, and I snap it shut. *It's really him.*

It's the stranger, as tall and tan and gorgeous as the night he blew into the Tiger Den and stopped time and space. In the past 60 hours I've imagined *him* in almost every place in town—but not here.

He walks to the desk in front of the room and sets down a stack of folders. Then he leans against the front of the desk, half-sitting, half-standing, and stares at us.

Miranda whispers, "That's the guy from New Year's! Remember?"

I remember.

Our principal, Ms. Wilcox, sticks her head into the room. "Everything all right, Mr. Wade?"

Wade. Mr. Wade. He has a name.

She doesn't wait for an answer and comes on in, stopping in front of the stranger and facing us. "Seniors, you may not have heard that Mrs. Overstreet won't be returning this semester."

I'm stunned. Helen Overstreet is an institution in Macon. She taught some of our parents in this very high school.

"Mrs. Overstreet suffered a slight stroke when she was visiting her sister in Des Moines over the holidays."

Chairs squeak. A few kids mutter things like *no way* and *wow*. I'm picturing Mrs. Overstreet in a hospital bed, reading Shakespeare. She loves Shakespeare.

"She's going to be just fine," Principal Wilcox continues, "but she's asked to take the rest of the year off to recuperate at her sister's. So she will be back with us next year, although *you* will not, with any luck."

We chuckle uneasily.

Principal Wilcox turns toward the stranger, who has been watching, the corners of his lips turned up so slightly, as if he's at the zoo observing the baboons. "We are fortunate enough to have been able to have hired a very qualified teacher to stand in and take over for our Mrs. Overstreet in her absence and in her hour of need. Mr. Mitchell Wade's excellent resumé stood out from among the many candidates we considered for this vital job."

She keeps talking, but my ears are pounding, thumping with blood rushing through my head. I was afraid I'd never see him again, and here he is in my high school, in my classroom.

" . . . all welcome Mitchell Wade, please?" Principal Wilcox taps her palm in applause, and

kyra's story

the front-row kids follow suit. Miranda and Tressa are clapping. Every girl in the room is.

I know I have to pull myself together.

The principal leaves, and Mitchell Wade follows her to the door, closes it, and leans back against it, facing us. "That woman can use more words to say less than anyone I've ever met," he says, shaking his head, his hair brushing his tanned forehead.

We laugh. We're merciless behind our principal's back. Sammy can do a perfect impersonation of an angry Principal Wilcox. But we're not used to teachers being in on it.

He walks to the window, braces his arms on the sill, and stares out at the snow-covered parking lot.

We don't speak. Kids shrug questions at each other. Tressa whispers something to me, but I don't get it.

Then he flips around, facing us again. "So this is Iowa."

He walks back to his desk—saunters, strolls, glides. I can't think of a word to describe how he moves, like he's not just from some other state but some other galaxy, where people don't need floors because they can tread on air.

He picks up the grade book, and for a second I'm so disappointed I want to cry. He's a teacher. Just a teacher with a grade book. But he opens it and stares at us, and I feel a surge of hope, as if something terrifying is about to happen.

"You . . . and I," he says, his gaze mowing us down, row by row, "are about to change, to alter one another's lives for all time."

He has us, every face turned to him, nobody breathing.

"We only have one semester, so we better get started."

Yes. Start. I believe him. I want to believe him.

4

"Miranda Sanchez?" This new teacher, this
Mr. Wade, says her name and looks up from the
grade book. He surveys the room until he spots
Miranda's raised finger. "Good," he says. But it
sounds like he means something more, and I feel
a pang of jealousy that surprises me.

"Jamal Jackson?" He's obviously not going
alphabetically, and I wonder how he's doing it,
picking out our names in some bizarre order only
he understands.

He calls every name except Sammy's and mine.

"Samuel James?" he says at last.

"That would be me." Sammy salutes him. "Call
me Sam."

The tanned stranger, our English teacher, turns
directly to me. Without regarding his grade book,

he calls out, "Samantha James." It's not a question.
I don't answer. "Any relation?" he asks, his expression not giving away whether or not he's kidding.

"Sammy's my baby brother," I explain, grateful
my mouth can still work and my voice isn't shaking, in spite of my heart jarring my rib cage. "Jeff
and Linda James are so efficient that they had us
on the same day and gave us approximately one
name between us. Fortunately, the hospital insisted
on filling in the middle name blank on our birth
certificates. Mine is Kyra, as in *KEY-rah*, and it's
what I go by."

I didn't mean to talk so much, but it's what I do
when I get nervous. Miranda clams up—I chatter. But
I know I don't sound nervous. Years of practice.

"You can call me *Mitch*," he says, still staring
back at me.

I think he's said this just to me, that *I* can call
him Mitch. But he smiles around the room and
repeats his invitation. "Please call me Mitch. Twenty
years from now, I'll happily respond to 'Mr. Wade.'
Right now though, Mr. Wade is my father."

I glance around the room and see that most of
us have scooted to the edge of our seats. Mrs. Overstreet would have called this a *cliché*.

Mitch, however, is no cliché. Everything he says,
everything he does, feels like the first time it's been
said or done in the history of humankind.

"I'd like to start our class with questions." He
pulls the teacher's wooden chair from behind the
desk and drags it a couple of feet in front of the first
row. I could kick myself for sitting in the back.

"Questions," he repeats, "*your* questions. Questions interest me much more than answers. I'd rather have you graduate knowing a few of the questions than have you leave high school knowing all the answers." He raises his eyebrows at us and waits.

Nobody's cutting up. There are no side conversations going on in this room.

Finally, Brianna Devereaux, who's been on the cheerleading squad as long as I have, asks, "Are you married?"

We laugh, but I'm waiting for the answer. I've never liked Brianna that much. I like her now.

Mitchell Wade—*Mitch*—stares at Brianna the whole time he answers her question. "No. Not married. I did have a girlfriend though."

I hear the word *did*, as in *don't now*.

"She was my housekeeper, you might say," he continues. "When I left, she *kept* the *house* we were living in."

Breathy little laughs dance around the room. I only know one couple who live together unmarried in Macon, and they're old. And Mitch is a teacher. I'm certain that the facts about his old girlfriend were left off of his excellent resumé.

I glance at Miranda but can't tell what she's thinking. Tressa, on the other hand, is an open magazine.

Manny raises his hand and waits for the nod from the teacher. He's our football star, headed for Iowa State on a big fat scholarship. "Where do you come from?" he asks.

"Laguna Beach . . . California," Mitch adds, like

we wouldn't know where Laguna Beach is. "Ever been to Laguna?"

"Not unless they've had a bowl game in the last four years," Manny answers. We all know his dad takes him to the Rose Bowl and Cotton Bowl every year.

"Best sunsets in the United States," Mitch says.

"Best tans, too, evidently," Tressa throws in.

I smile at her and see her cheeks have turned blotchy red.

"Why did you come to Macon?" Jamal asks. "You got family in Iowa or what?"

Mitch smiles at him, showing us the whitest teeth in Iowa. "I believe everyone should have a close-knit, loving, and caring family . . . and keep them in another state."

Appreciative chuckles snake across the room.

"What's left of my family is in Washington and New York. No, no family here. I'll need friends though." He gives us his toothpaste-commercial smile again. He means he needs friends and we're to be it. He wants *us* to be his friends.

Who is he?

Miranda looks to me, waiting. Jason and Dan turn around and shoot me looks. I know they expect me to ask a choice question.

I can think of a million things I want to know about Mitchell Wade, including how he feels about dating younger women. I start to ask his age when he pulls something out of his sports jacket. The jacket is blended wool, subtle and expensive. It covers a deep brown turtleneck cable sweater. He turns around and fires a baseball to Tony on the front row.

Tony catches it, even though he's the one you'd choose last in a game of pickup ball.

"Happy New Year," Mitch says evenly. "Right?" It sounds like a challenge the way he says it, and we don't take the challenge. "When you've got the ball," Mitch explains, "I want you to give us one of your New Year's resolutions before tossing the ball back to me. Tony?" He must have remembered Tony's name from roll call. Mrs. Overstreet didn't know Tony's name after three years with him in class.

Tony is a lucky first pick on Mitch's part. He's the kind of guy who's probably written down 20 resolutions in priority order and drawn little boxes beside each one to be checked off when accomplished.

But Tony surprises us, or maybe he doesn't feel like revealing his list of resolutions. "I had a good year last year. I intend to stay the course this year, to keep myself on the right track to where I'm going." He tosses the ball back.

Mitch's forehead gets a wrinkle between his eyebrows. "Even if you're on the right track, Tony, you'll get run over if you just sit there."

He whips the ball to Tyrone, who doesn't return Mitch's smile. "Do my best. That's about it." Tyrone fires the ball back. The snap of the ball into Mitch's hand sounds like a slap. I wonder why I ever went out with Tyrone Larson.

Mitch returns Tyrone's glare with a grin. "Only the mediocre are at their best, Tyrone."

The game continues. I think he's going to throw me the ball, but instead, it goes to Josh Hertzog, the biggest tackle on the Macon Tiger team, who says he resolves to lose weight.

Mitch knows the names of everyone he tosses the ball to, and he's not even glancing into the grade book. I'm waiting for my turn, wanting him to toss that ball to me.

"Tressa?" He lobs the ball to her. She drops it, and Drew retrieves it for her, placing it in the palm of her hand.

"I don't know." She's acting the dizzy, red-headed cheerleader for him. "Maybe this year I'll finally keep up with the Joneses." She smiles at me. Am I the Joneses?

I can't take it anymore. I haven't said word one since Mitchell Wade started playing ball. "No way, Tressa!" I deliver a tiny punch to her arm. "Don't keep up with the Joneses! Drag them down with you, girl! Much more fun!"

She giggles, but I get a burst of laughter from the crowd.

Okay, Mitch. My turn. Give me the ball.

He ignores me and throws his stupid ball to Jenna . . . I can't even think of her last name. I'm pretty sure she's gone to school here since elementary, but she never talks—in class or out—that I can remember. She's bone-thin, with a long face that reminds me of Popeye's Olive Oyl. Gran would have said she could eat an apple through a picket fence.

Jenna turns the ball in her hands as if it's a

crystal ball, holding her future. Softly she says, "I resolve not to have another year like last year."

A couple of kids laugh. Someone says, "I'll second that!"

But a shiver of sadness shoots through me, and I wonder if something has happened to Jenna that we don't know about or if it's the regular stuff we do know about, maybe even that we do. I don't want to think about it, so I stop thinking for as long as I can.

More kids catch the ball. More resolutions are revealed. Each time I'm sure Mitch will toss the ball to me, but it's like he can't see me. What am I? Invisible?

Rebecca Landis leans forward to snatch the ball out of the air. She's our girl jock, the best player on the girls' basketball team. "Finally!" she exclaims, her brown ponytail swinging.

"Rebecca?" Mitch grins at her. "What's your best New Year's resolution?"

"Thought you'd never ask . . . *Mitch*." She's trying it on for size, his first name.

We steal glances to see if the new teacher reacts. He doesn't.

"Okay." Rebecca scooches straight up in her seat, as if she's aiming for a free throw. "I resolve *only* to date *real* gentlemen." She frowns around the room. "Got that, guys?"

We laugh. But Mitch wants more. "And exactly what *is* a real gentleman, Rebecca?"

That knocks the wind out of her. Here she's been forming her clever answer in her head the whole time. Now she's out of comebacks.

I speak up, not missing a beat. "A gentleman is someone who knows how to play the accordion and the ukulele, but doesn't." Even *I'm* not sure what I mean, but I pull it off, totally straight-faced, faking deep wisdom and meaning.

The class divides and livens up. Some say I've hit it exactly and anyone who doesn't get it is obviously not a gent. Others say I'm putting them on or I'm just crazy.

Mitch motions to Rebecca to toss the ball back, and he throws it immediately to Brent. I think Mitch is ignoring me on purpose now, and I don't like it.

"Exercise more," Brent says. He's in decent shape, a benchwarmer on the basketball team. I think his real resolution is to get more game time before he graduates. Brent's okay. If I were Coach, I'd give him the game time, even without a resolution.

"Maybe I can help you there, Brent," says our leader. "I bought the bike shop on East Main. I'll be biking every morning before school and most afternoons after, unless the roads are too icy. You're welcome to join me." Mitch looks up from his private chat with Brent. "You're all invited."

Lots of kids say, "Cool!" and "All right, man!"

I hate the way all of this is making me feel, like I'm on the outside. No, this I do not like.

Tressa, who probably hasn't been on a bike since fourth grade, chimes in, "Biking is really great for the calves. Super exercise."

"Exercise, bah humbug," I comment. "I'm against anything that makes people smell."

Sammy flings his pencil at me, and Mitch tosses the ball to him. "Sam?"

"I will not criticize—" he cranes his neck around to look at me pointedly—"or *be* criticized by people—" he turns back to face Mitch again—"unless we've walked a mile in each other's moccasins." Sammy stands up and takes a bow.

The room applauds.

"Unless you walk a mile in my brother's moccasins," I mutter, making sure it comes out loud enough for Mitch to hear, "you cannot imagine the smell."

That one gets me the best laughs of the morning. But I feel like I've been working overtime to get there. And Mitch still acts like he isn't hearing me.

Every student in our class has gotten the ball and given a resolution except for Jeremy Stanwick and me.

Jeremy looks almost fearful, cringing in the far corner in the back of the room, hugging the wall, two seats from the nearest student. I'm not surprised when Mitch lobs the ball to him or when Jeremy drops it and the ball thuds to the floor and rolls a couple of feet before he can trap it and sit back down.

The wall clock says two minutes of class left.

Jeremy clears his throat. "I want to get out of Macon, Iowa." His voice drops. "But I won't. I can't."

The room goes silent—maybe because it's what we'd all say if we had the guts. Maybe it's because Jeremy is so pleading, so pitiful. I want to go over to him and give him a hug and promise he'll get out and have a wonderful life and a family who will always love him and children who will talk to him, *really* talk.

Mitch walks to that side of the room. "Jeremy, don't say you can't. You can."

"If you have money, you can," Jeremy says. It's a rare contradiction from a guy who rarely gives any opinion, who holds up the cafeteria line because he can't decide on white or chocolate milk.

"You can always find some way out," Mitch says, his stare forcing Jeremy to look at him, like a magnet drawing metal shavings. "There's more than one way to skin a cat, you know."

I think I see Jeremy shrink or melt into his chair. Nobody makes a sound, and I want to cover the silence, to at least give him a way out of this, if not out of Macon.

"Well—" my voice sounds loud—"if there really *is* more than one way to skin a cat, I for one do not want to hear about it."

The spell is broken. We're back to laughing, and Jeremy becomes invisible again.

The bell rings. We start to get up. Chairs screech.

But Mitch acts like he doesn't hear it. He throws the ball to me.

I catch it.

Nobody moves. Some sit back down. Others stand by their desks.

"I resolve to only dread one day at a time," I say. It's a Woody Allen line, and it works for me here like it did for Woody.

Kids chuckle and make for the crowded halls.

I'm still sitting, holding the ball. Miranda and Tressa walk out, not together. I wait for the room to clear. Then I take the ball to the front of the room and place it into Mitchell Wade's hands.

I turn to go.

"I figured you liked Woody Allen," he says.

I look back over my shoulder, wondering if I've imagined this.

Mitch's brown eyes pierce me the way they did at the Tiger Den. He remembers. I can see that.

"But dreading every day," he says, "one day at a time . . . I think you mean that, Kyra."

By lunch, I've replayed my scene with Mitch
a million times in my head. Sometimes I rewrite it,
giving myself a perfect comeback line. Sometimes
he takes me into his arms when he says, "But
dreading every day . . . I think you mean that,
Kyra," and we both cry, determining to face the
world together.

"Iowa calling Kyra James?" Shawna, Jamal's
sister, eyes me across the lunch table.

"Sorry." I take a bite of my apple, the only
thing I'm eating from my tray. "I was thinking
about all that econ work Hatt gave us." Actually,
I finished the work in class while he was laying
out the semester plan.

D.J. takes a seat across from me, flanked by
Manny and Dave, football seniors. Two of my fellow

cheerleaders are giggling at the end of the table. Around us, silverware clangs and voices crash into each other. I'm already getting a headache.

"I am going to hate that class!" Shawna complains. It's a second before I remember we're still talking about econ. Shawna is a junior and probably the smartest junior in our school. Jamal told Sammy his sister is going to med school when she graduates, and I believe it.

"On the other hand," I say, trying to keep up my end of the conversation, "it *is* all about money, right? How bad can that be?"

D.J. hasn't said anything, but I've caught him sneaking peeks in my direction.

I give him a good once-over now. He's wearing tight jeans with exactly the right shirt, a cream color that makes his brown eyes even dreamier. The guy is definitely ripped. Every girl who walks by our table—and some have zigzagged the long way through the cafeteria to pass by—touches D.J. on the shoulder or says hey to him.

I can't even remember why I've been giving him a hard time. "Great shirt, D.J.," I say with meaning.

He looks up, his spaghetti-laden fork stalled in midair.

"Sweet! Get it for Christmas?" I ask, helping him out.

He swallows and nods. "Yeah."

"Very cool. Very you." I've gotten all the mileage I can out of his new shirt. "So, any of your classes shaping up to be tolerable?" *Rephrase.* "Good ones?"

I feel Tressa staring at me. No doubt she liked it better when I was leaving D.J. alone.

"Shop," D.J. says.

"I *love* shopping!" I say, grinning. He doesn't grin back, so I make the save. "Oh, stupid me! Shop! Like making things out of wood and stuff? Will they show you how to make bookcases, do you think? Or video stands or CD racks? I am totally out of space in my room."

D.J. sets down his fork. He has a drop of spaghetti on the side of his mouth. I take my napkin, lean across the table, and wipe it off for him. His head automatically jerks back. Then he holds still while I rub off the red blob. "There," I say, going back to my apple.

He hasn't answered my question about bookcases. But I can tell he's working up to something. "Wanna get something to eat after school, Kyra?" he blurts out.

I reward him with my best smile. "Sure." I stop eating my apple.

The second of victory, that instant rush of satisfaction at having gotten D.J. to ask me out again—well, maybe not out, but it counts—vanishes as fast as it came.

Tressa is trying to pretend she hasn't been listening, but I can tell she's faking. She asks Shawna about world history class.

Miranda doesn't look up from her plate the entire lunch period. I probably should ask her what's wrong, but I'm not sure I can handle one more problem, even if it belongs to someone else.

Manny pitches his empty milk carton, which really isn't even a carton anymore but a silver bag with a straw, into the wastebasket and sinks it.

"Sure you don't want to go out for basketball, Manny?" I ask him.

"Man," he says, not answering my question, "what did you think of that dude . . . *Mitch*?" He says *Mitch* like it's a magic word and he half expects a puff of smoke to envelop us.

I shrug. "Jury's not out on him." In my head, I still hear his voice telling me I mean that, about dreading every day.

"I think the guy's cool," Manny says. He tells the rest of the lunch crew about our tall tan Mitch and his baseball routine.

My head is starting to throb now, and Manny's voice grates on me. Someone has turned up the volume on the cafeteria soundtrack.

"Anybody have aspirin?" I ask. I think I interrupted Manny in mid-sentence. He's wide-eyed, mouth open, with elbows on the table and finger pointed.

"Where've *you* been?" Tressa asks, sharper than she meant because she tries softening it with a sweet smile. But I know she's mad about D.J. I'll call her tonight and make it all right. But right now I just want to get rid of the vise closing around my head.

"If I gave you—or *me,* for that matter—one lousy aspirin," Tressa continues, "I'd get us both kicked out of school."

She's right, and I know it. But it still makes me

mad. I mean, like a couple of aspirin will turn us into addicts?

But I know aspirin wouldn't do much for me anyway.

■   ■   ■

By the time our first day of our last semester of high school is over, word of Mitchell Wade has filtered into every cranny of our school. He is now "the surfer teacher." He's also "Mr. Cool," "DDG—Drop Dead Gorgeous," and just *Mitch*. Even the janitor stops and asks me if I met the new teacher.

"I met him, Mr. Clean," I answer. It's his actual name—honest. He's been our maintenance man since seventh grade. I think he's one of the few people I'll actually miss from Macon High.

Before going to my locker to meet up with D.J., I spot Sammy and Tyrone by Sammy's locker. "Sammy!" I yell.

He turns around, and I'm struck with how much he's starting to look like our dad—not Dad now, but in the old pictures—solid, dependable, strong chin. I make a mental note not to let Sammy turn into Dad, at least not yet. Girls love Sammy, but he doesn't take enough advantage of that fact. I don't mean take advantage of *them*. I just mean he's missing out by being such a straight arrow.

Sammy waves and hoists his bookbag over his shoulder.

When I walk up to them, they stop talking. I don't like the way Tyrone openly eyes me head to toe. Like I'm for sale, used, and he's thinking about kicking my tires.

"Need a ride home, Sis?" Sammy asks. He gave me a ride in the morning because my car, a '92, past-its-prime Grand Prix, is still in the shop getting new brakes. I'm not that crazy about driving anyway.

"No, thanks. That's why I wanted to catch you." I think about asking him what's up with Tyrone, who's watching us like we're TV. But D.J.'s waiting on me. "I got another ride. See you later."

He shuts his locker. The click echoes in the emptying halls and reminds me of my headache. It's stopped throbbing and turned into a steady, nagging, echoing pain.

"Later!" Sammy yells, trotting down the hall after Tyrone. It's Dad's trot.

■   ■   ■

Did I say that D.J. drives a rebuilt Mustang, a mint '68? It's definitely part of his charm. He's standing beside it, and I notice that his shirt matches the cream-colored car exactly. I wonder if he's gotten the shirt on purpose, to match his Mustang. What would Vin Diesel do?

Three sophomore cheerleaders are hanging around D.J. like flies on sweetbread, Gran would have said. One of them, Ann Marie, notices me and waves. "Hey, Kyra! Great car, huh? Lucky you!"

I smile. Lucky me.

D.J. opens the driver's door and has me slide in

first, his brand of chivalry. I fasten my seat belt. I've ridden with him enough to know I'd better.

"So, burgers and fries?" he asks, rubbing a smudge off the dash with his shirtsleeve. He starts the engine and backs out of the seniors' parking lot. Gravel crunches. I smell stale cigarettes in his ash-tray, and I think I might be sick.

All I can think about is the homework I need to do. We're having a quiz in history on Friday. I want to work ahead so I don't fall behind once cheerlead-ing and play practice kick in. Next week I'll be miss-ing a day of school when Dad takes us to NYU to check out housing, and we have a French test that day.

I can't do it. "D.J.," I say, holding an index finger to my temple. I can feel the blood throbbing there.

"Huh?"

"Would you be really upset with me if I asked you to just take me home?"

"Huh?"

"I've got the linebacker of all headaches." *Basket-ball, not football.* "I mean, it feels like a whole team is dribbling basketballs inside my skull. I need to take some aspirin and lie down."

He frowns over at me. The car wanders into the wrong lane. "You really have a headache?" He jerks the car back into our lane.

"Can Vince Carter dunk? Can Jordan jump? Can Shaq attack?" I ask, glad I did my basketball home-work.

"Yeah. Okay." But I can tell he only half-believes me. *I* only half-believe me. Even without the headache, I don't think I would have been up for more food with D.J. I probably would have faked a headache.

"Listen," I say, as he turns up Oak Street, cruising through a yellow-red light and speeding up at the deer crossing. I'm not too worried. In 17 years I've seen only half a dozen deer take advantage of their crossing. "Let's do something this weekend, okay?"

His face is so transparent—handsome, but wide-open spaces. "Yeah? Okay. Like a movie or something like that?"

"Great." I'm not thinking *great*. And I'm hoping Vin doesn't make a new movie between now and then. But I don't have a date for the weekend yet. And it *is* my last semester of high school.

6

D.J. swerves his Mustang to the curb in front of my house and jerks to a stop.

I pop the seat belt and make a clean getaway. "Thanks for the ride, D.J.," I say through the closed window. "And for being so understanding. Can't wait for the weekend."

He nods and takes off as soon as I stand back.

The garage door is shut, so Mom's not home yet. Good. I need solitude to study. I stand on the side-walk and fish through my bag for the house key.

"Kyra! Look at me!"

I turn to see Bethany on her big, three-wheel bike. She's wearing a ski jacket and stocking mask, both purple, her favorite color. The Grays bought her the bike when she was seven because they knew she'd never be able to balance a two-wheeler and

neighbor kids were already making fun of her train-
ing wheels. So they got this great bike that even
grown-ups use, with a basket in front and behind.
And Bethany's bike was suddenly the envy of every
kid on our block.

"You rock, Bethany!" I shout.

"Watch me, Kyra!" she yells back. She pedals
faster toward me. Her sidewalk is perfectly shoveled,
clean and dry, and I know her big brother's respon-
sible.

Dylan steps out of their garage and hollers,
"Bethany! Hold up! I got your gloves." He jogs after
her, but she keeps coming at me, her bare hands
clutching the bike handlebars.

I run up the walk to her and stick out my palm
like a crossing guard. "Hey, young lady! Halt in the
name of the law! Speed limit is only 100 miles an
hour around these parts."

Bethany stops a foot from me and crumples with
laughter over the handlebars.

Dylan walks up and sticks her gloves on for her.
"How was your first day, Kyra?" he asks, tugging
fingers into wool.

"Okay, I guess." My headache has lifted to a dull
pressure at the base of my neck. I feel freeze-dried.

"Did you like the new English teacher? Wade?
You have him first hour, right?"

I nod, wondering if Dylan will be the only one
not to call him Mitch. "When do you have him?"

"Fourth." Dylan tugs at Bethany's cap until both
of her eyes match the holes. Inside the house their
dog's barking like crazy.

I'm starting to feel the cold, so I stamp my feet. "Did he do that baseball/New Year's resolution thing with you guys?" I ask.

"Nope. I heard about it, though. He read to us for half of the class—existential stuff, Sartre and Camus." Dylan's ears are pink. He's wearing his school jacket but no hat. "I thought you and D.J. didn't hit it off."

I was wondering if he'd seen D.J. drop me off. I shrug. "He's okay."

Dylan doesn't say anything. Dylan Gray never says anything too bad about anybody, at least not behind their backs. But he's no pushover either. He doesn't mind speaking his piece in front of you.

"Let's go!" Bethany cries, turning her handlebars so sharp the bike won't pedal.

Dylan runs to the rescue.

"See you guys!" I call after them. Then I hustle to the front door, unlock it, and go in.

Our house smells like a mixture of cinnamon and lavender. It's no accident. Mom selects the smell of the month from a potpourri shop in Clarinda.

The living room is dark, with curtains drawn, but light streams in from the kitchen and dining room. We live on one of the nicer streets in Macon. The best houses, the biggest houses, are over by the golf course. If Macon were a city, our street would proba-bly be one of the good suburbs.

Most of the houses in our block look alike. It used to freak me out to go into Dylan's house because the layout is backwards from ours. His stairs are to the right of the kitchen and the kitchen is on the left of the dining room, instead of the other way around. And upstairs, the bedrooms are turned around and the bathroom is on the wrong side.

My favorite thing in our house is the fireplace. We used to fire it up a lot. Now it's down to Christmas Eve, and this year we didn't even have a fire then. Dylan's family has a fire almost every night in the winter. I know because I see the smoke from their chimney and open my bedroom window to smell it.

I fling my bookbag on the dining-room table and pull out every book for every class. I can't see over the stack, and a panic seeps in through the pores of my skin. Staring at the pile of books, I feel as if I have to read all of them now. I know I don't. And I know it's stupid to feel this way. But I can't help it. My chest feels like the stack of texts is sitting on it, pressing down harder and harder.

I don't know where to start, so I begin with my first class and plan to move through assignments class by class. Mitch didn't really give us an assignment, so I start with the first chapter in our lit book anyway.

But in my head, I hear Mitch's voice: *Dreading every day, one day at a time . . . I think you mean that, Kyra.*

The phone rings, and I catch it before the second ring. "Hello?"

"Have you checked your aluminum siding lately? Right now in your neighborhood we have a special sale—"

I slam the receiver down, angry at the interruption. Then I take the phone off the hook and leave it.

Switching to French, I review vocabulary lists. I've aced two semesters of French, but the third is supposed to be the hardest.

When I finish the lists, I keep my book open so I can review more after I read our history assignment.

Suddenly I remember the housing form I'm supposed to fill out for NYU before Friday. Only I can't remember where I put it. I scour my bag, check the house mail pile, the magazine rack, the counters. But it's nowhere.

Checking my bedroom, I imagine getting to NYU without it. I can't say I've lost the form. I'll be branded as an airhead before I even enroll.

But the form isn't upstairs or downstairs. And I resign myself to waiting until Mom gets home so I can ask her. Only I don't want to ask her because she's big on responsibility. Sammy's the irresponsible one. Not me.

I try to get back to business with my history book. There are so many dates and names, all possible quiz material.

The doorbell rings.

I stay where I am, out of sight of the front windows. I cannot afford another interruption.

Someone knocks and rings again.

I cover my ears and try to read about Egypt and the Pharaohs.

But it's not working. And the pounding grows louder and louder.

I cross the room toward the door and hear Dylan. He's yelling.

"Kyra! Help! It's Bethany!" He's kicking the door.

I fumble with the latch and open the door.

Dylan's standing there, holding Bethany like a baby in his arms. The purple sleeve of her coat is shoved up to her elbow, and something white is tied around her arm. But the white is turning red fast. And blood drips from her arm and pools in the snow on our step.

I stare at the puddle of blood on the step. My hand won't release the doorknob. Bethany's losing blood. Lots of it.

"Kyra, we have to get her to the hospital. Now! I can't wait for the ambulance." Dylan runs to his car in the driveway.

I race after him. Bethany turns her head to see me. She tries to grin, but her eyes show pain. She's limp in Dylan's arms.

I pass Dylan and open the back door of his car so he can lay Bethany on the seat.

"Hey, Bethie." I slide in, then shift to the other side so I can cradle her head and arms in my lap. "Didn't I tell you not to do 100 miles an hour on that hot rod of yours?"

Dylan lunges into the driver's seat, glances back,

his face contorted. "This will be faster. Just keep pressure on the tourniquet." He slams his door and starts the car.

"I'm sorry," Bethany says.

I smooth her hair, then pull the bright red bandage tighter. I'm afraid to speak. I don't want her to know how scared I am. Bethany is a bleeder. If she were a male, she'd be a hemophiliac. Even a little cut can mean real danger.

"You're doing fine, Bethie!" Dylan says, his voice controlled, regular-sounding. It's amazing the way he gathers himself for her. "Dr. Marchand loves seeing you. She'll probably thank you for coming to the hospital, you know. You're her favorite patient."

Wide-eyed, Bethany turns to me. "Dr. Marchand always says, 'Here's my favorite patient.'"

"I'm not surprised," I say, pressing my fingers on the bandage. Blood throbs out in thin streaks.

"Dylan," Bethany whispers, biting her lip. I see the space between her front teeth. "It hurts, and my head feels funny."

"Almost there, kid," Dylan says, pressing the accelerator. "Want to talk to Jesus, Bethie? *I* sure do. Help us out here, please. We could really use a parking spot, too. And for Dr. Marchand to be in the building."

For a minute I think Dylan's asking *me* about parking spots. His voice is so natural, so normal that it can't be prayer. But I've forgotten how real Dylan's Jesus is.

"Thanks for making Bethie so brave," Dylan continues, swerving into the hospital emergency lot.

"And thanks for that spot!" He pulls into an empty parking space next to the emergency entrance.

"Amen!" Bethany says.

My heart, or something inside of me, pounds in tiny beats, making my throat and chest quiver. The blood keeps coming from Bethany's tiny arm. I want to ask Jesus to make it stop—forget the parking place and stop the bleeding. I want to ask Jesus a lot of things, but he feels too far away.

Dylan opens the back door and hands me his cell phone. "I'll get her," he says, leaning in the second I step out. "Call my mom at work. Tell her where we are and that Bethie's okay. And not to worry."

Two men in white run out to the car as Dylan lifts Bethany out of the backseat.

"Are you cut? Shot?" asks the skinny man with glasses, taking my arm. He's staring at my stomach.

I look down and see that I'm covered in blood.

"No!" Dylan says. "It's Bethany! She's a bleeder. She needs Dr. Marchand."

He signals to the other attendant, who says something into a walkie-talkie thing. A stretcher bursts from the glass emergency doors, but Dylan isn't waiting. He storms past it and on into the hospital. We run after him.

"Did you get Dr. Marchand?" he shouts. "Bethany needs an IV and desmopressin and maybe fresh plasma. Now!"

"Dr. Marchand is on her way," says the bigger attendant, the one without glasses. His voice is calm. "Let's get her to a bed where she can lie down, okay?"

Dylan carries Bethany and follows a nurse, who leads them to a cubicle with curtains for walls to separate us from the other emergencies.

A young woman in a blue lab coat rushes up and goes straight for Bethany's arm. "Hello. Dr. Marchand is on the way. I'm Dr. Cellars. What happened here, young lady?" She has a nice voice and smiles at Bethany.

"I fell off my bike," Bethany answers, wincing as Dr. Cellars unties the bandage. Blood shoots out, and she reties the tourniquet.

"Someone did a nice job on this bandage," she says, turning to me.

"Dylan." I sound hoarse, out of breath. I can't stop shaking.

She turns to Dylan. "Are you her–?"

"Brother," Dylan answers. "She needs an IV of desmopress–"

"Well, look who we have here!" A tiny dark-skinned woman walks in, parting the curtains. Her black hair is pulled back straight in a band. "Ah, here's my favorite patient." She winks at Dylan and goes to Bethany. "What have we done to this arm?"

"I fell off my bike," Bethany explains.

"Bicycle? In this weather? Ai-i-i!"

The doctor mutters orders to the nurse and to Dr. Cellars, who nod and take off in opposite directions. They're back in seconds with a tray of instruments, a metal pole, and a sack of clear fluid.

"This won't hurt much, and I know how brave my favorite patient is." Dr. Marchand inserts a needle into Bethany's good arm and connects a plastic tubing that runs to the clear fluid in the bag. The nurse takes the bag and hangs it over the metal pole.

"Bethany," Dr. Marchand says, her face inches from Bethany's, "do you mind if I ask your brother and your friend to wait out in the waiting room while we get you fixed up?"

"That's okay," Bethany says. She turns so she can see Dylan. "You should call Mom and Dad."

I gasp, staring at the cell in my hand. "I'm sorry! I—I forgot." How could I have forgotten? Couldn't I have done even that one thing for them? I feel worse than useless—guilty.

Dylan takes the phone and puts his arm around my shoulder. "Are you sure she's okay?" he asks the doctor. "I was afraid to wait for the ambulance after what happened last time."

"I would have done the same, Dylan, as close as you are to the hospital. Bethany will be fine now. We've started the IV. The desmopressin will help the blood coagulate. We have plasma ready if we need it, but I don't think we will. You go call your parents now—but *outside* with that cell phone."

I feel like I'm going to faint. Dylan's arm tightens around me.

"We'll be right outside, in the waiting room, if you need us though," Dylan says.

"And I think you may have to buy your girlfriend a new sweater," Dr. Marchand says.

We take the only two empty seats in a closet-sized waiting room next to a woman in a cast and across from a man with bloodshot eyes. Dylan steps outside to call his parents, and time stops until he comes back.

He takes the chair next to me. "Hated to leave this on the answering machine, but they'll check it as soon as they get home. Mom's already left work, and Dad must be in the car. He forgets to turn on his cell."

He leans down, his elbows on his knees. His hands clasp around the back of his neck.

I wonder if he's praying. Envy slices through me like a warm knife. I can almost see his muscles relax and the tension ease as his fingers loosen around his neck.

When he sits up, he smiles at me. "Thanks, Kyra. For a minute there, I didn't think you were going to answer your door. And your line was busy. But you came through for me—for Bethany."

A wave of guilt washes over me. I'd left the phone off the hook on purpose. And I should have opened the door right away. "Sorry, Dylan." It comes out a whisper.

He grins at my new, once-white Christmas sweater. "Actually, I'm the sorry one. We'll get you another sweater."

I punch his arm. "Yeah—that's what I'm all about. Get me a new sweater."

He laughs. We sit like that for a while. A little boy on the couch in the corner is crying, but I can't see anything wrong with him. He's with an older girl and a man in a one-piece work suit and work boots. "Bob" is printed on the man's shirt pocket.

"I have to see if she's okay." Dylan stands up and

walks to the glass partition separating the sick and well. He has to talk the receptionist into it, but she finally lets him through. He waves a hand at me as he slips out of the waiting room, headed for Bethany.

I'm glad he's going to be with his sister. I try not to look at the others in the waiting room. I have the most blood on me, but I feel guilty for taking up space here, as if I'm just faking tragedy and using Bethany's blood as my stage prop, while they're all here legit, with real emergencies and injuries.

"Bethany Gray? We're her parents. Is she all right? We need to see her!" Mr. and Mrs. Gray are at the reception desk.

I get up and run over to them. "She's okay!" I shout.

"Kyra!" Mr. Gray shouts back.

Mrs. Gray runs up to me. Her face is red and her makeup smeared. "Kyra, where is she? Where's Dylan?" She stares at my bloody sweater and covers her mouth with one hand.

"Bethany's okay. Dylan's with her." I fill them in on as much as I can, while a nurse leads all of us back to the curtained emergency room.

The curtain parts on Bethany, Dylan, and Dr. Marchand. Mr. Gray takes his wife's hand before they step inside.

"Very nice," Mr. Gray says, totally erasing the fear from his voice. I see where Dylan gets it. "I should have known you two would cook up some way to throw a party without us." He kisses Bethany on the forehead. "How's it going, Peaches?"

"I fell off my bike, Daddy," Bethany says.

"I heard. You doing okay, now?"

"I'm fine," Bethany says. Her face is white, though. Clear liquid drips into the tube and vibrates down into her sticklike arm. A clean bandage covers her wound.

Mrs. Gray takes the opposite side of the bed and holds her daughter's hand.

"I will second that," Dr. Marchand says. "Bethany is fine. We have the bleeding just about stopped. Dylan and this young lady got Bethany here so fast, I think we won't even need a transfusion. But I would like to keep her with me for a while. She *is* my favorite patient, you know."

Bethany giggles.

I watch them as if I'm on the opposite side of a TV screen. I can't help wondering how our family would have handled it if Sammy or I had been born with Down's syndrome and the daily trauma of a Bethany.

■　　■　　■

By the time Dylan drives me home, it's dark and my head aches again, worse than before. We turn onto our street, and I catch a flash of Dylan's face in the green light of his blinker. He has the profile of a man . . . not a kid, not a high school guy.

He catches me staring at him. "What?"

I shake my head.

"What, Kyra?"

"How do you do it?" I ask. "And your parents? How can you all take it?"

He pulls into his driveway and leaves the motor running. Then he turns to me with intense, narrow, brown eyes. "We don't know each other very well anymore, Kyra. But I think you know the answer to that one, how we get through this stuff with Bethany."

I know what he's going to say, and I don't want to hear it. God. Jesus. My head feels like it weighs more than my body. I undo my seat belt and take the easier half of his answer. "Dylan, how can you say we don't know each other, you idiot?" I open the door. "I know *you* like a book—a cheesy novel, to be exact." I get out and close the door. "Call me and let me know how Bethany is!"

I make a dash for my house. Light glows from inside. I open the door and smell Chinese take-out. They're home. TV's on. My books and homework are still hogging the table. The NYU housing form is set out for me on one end. And I'd give anything if all of it would just go away.

8

Thursday night we fly out of Des Moines, bound for New York. On the plane, I work on advanced algebra, while Sammy sleeps and our parents read. When we land, snow swirls around runway ramps, and huge flakes dance in beams of light, signaling us in.

Friday morning I call Miranda and report in as promised. "With any luck, I'll get snowed in here and miss another day of school." But I'm faking it. I can't afford to miss another day and have more work to make up.

Dad makes sure I meet every NYU theater prof who's not nailed down out of our reach. I want to get excited about college, the way Dylan does when he talks about Iowa State. But all I can see as we walk the campus are girls who are prettier and more talented than I'll ever be.

■ ■ ■

Friday afternoon we split up and agree to meet for
dinner at the pizza place by our hotel. When I wan-
der into the dimly lit restaurant, I see Mom and Dad
right off. They're leaning across the checkered table-
cloth, whispering in short, sharp bursts. I stay where
I am and watch them.

My parents never argue. They're too polite to
argue.

When I join them, they stop and greet me with
smiles. For the next half hour, they talk to me but
not to each other. They sigh at each other—short
sighs and long, breathy ones, sighs that cut the air
like steel. I've heard them all before. I call it *sigh
language.* It's as if the two of them have their own
language, and I could understand them if I could
just crack the code.

My stomach is so tied up I know I won't be able
to eat. "Where's Sammy?" I ask.

"I don't know." Dad waves for the waiter. "But
we're not waiting any longer. Sausage and onion
good for everybody?"

Mom clears her throat, a technique sometimes
employed to punctuate sighs. "Sammy went to a
music store, I believe." Her forehead is a map of
worry lines. "He should have been back by now."
She peers toward the window. "I hope nothing's
happened to him."

Dad answers with a long sigh, which Mom counters with a huff.

"You know, Kyra," Dad says, surveying the room

filled with young New Yorkers, "I've always wanted to live in New York. I hope you realize how lucky you are."

I smile and agree. But I'm feeling less lucky with every tick of the pizza-shaped wall clock. The NYU coeds and the stylish women eating sushi at the bar make me feel 12, with braces and baby fat.

Mom sighs again, and I think Dad's staring too much at the long-legged brunettes at the next table. Then I feel even worse for thinking it, because he's not like that.

I hear a snap and turn to see Mom opening her leather purse. She pulls it into her lap and comes out with an orange plastic bottle. Dad sighs, and Mom sighs back as she takes out one pill, places it on her tongue, and takes a sip of water.

I don't think much about it until maybe 15 minutes later. Sammy still hasn't shown, and Mom should be much more anxious, since he's almost an hour late now. But she's not. Instead, smiling, she reaches under the table to hold Dad's hand. She's not even sighing.

Sammy comes in with a college girl on his arm, and Mom chuckles about it instead of reading him the riot act. Even her face is different—smooth and flushed.

We have a nice meal and then walk back to our hotel, my parents holding hands. I've seen Mom take pills before. I've even seen that orange bottle, or one like it, in their medicine cabinet back home. But I can't stop wondering now, marveling really.

At the hotel, Sammy and I change into our

swimsuits, and Mom and Dad go down to the hotel lounge to listen to old people's piano music.

"Okay, Sis. Ready to hit the pool?" Sammy snaps me with a white towel and races out the door.

I grab a towel and start after him when I glimpse Mom's purse lying on a chair by the door. Sammy's already down the hall and out of sight. Slowly I shut the door and pick up the purse. The orange bottle is sitting there in plain sight. I take it out and hold it under the lamp to read the label: *Zanax. Caution: May be habit-forming.*

The cap comes off easily when I match the arrows, and I shake out one pill. It looks kind of like an aspirin. I get water from the bathroom and swallow the pill.

I wait, but nothing happens. I've heard kids talk about drugs and how different they make you feel. I've been to more than a couple of parties where kids smoked pot. But this is nothing like that. I'm not even tipsy, or dizzy. I've gotten that way a couple of times in my 17 years—once with Sammy when we were 15 and our parents were gone. We both hurled and retreated to our separate rooms to sleep it off. Another time was with a guy I met last summer, and I swore I'd never get drunk again after that.

I honestly think the stupid Zanax doesn't work on me, that it must just be for old people. Disenchanted, I head down to the pool.

Sammy's already swimming with a couple of younger kids. I dive into the water and come up again. Only it feels like I'm still underwater, deep and surrounded by crystals of water and bubbles. Yet I can breathe and see clearly.

I float on my back, but I'm convinced I wouldn't need the water to hold me. My head clears, like the water, and school and NYU, my parents, and even Sammy are nothing but imagination as I drift.

For a good 20 minutes I believe that I have never felt so good, or so peaceful, in my whole life.

■   ■   ■

Monday I'm back in the real world of Macon, Iowa, where a make-up test and who-knows-what-else are waiting for me at school.

"Kyra, have some breakfast." Mom's path has crossed mine in the kitchen. Dad's reading the paper by the winter sunlight streaming through the window.

I'm on the fly, anxious to get to school early. "I already ate. Thanks."

I haven't eaten, and I wouldn't need to lie about it. Mom might give me the health lecture, or maybe toss me an apple. That's it. But I lie anyway. I've been doing it without thinking lately.

"When are they going to decide on a new drama coach for the senior play?" Mom asks. "Shouldn't you start rehearsing pretty soon?"

"I'm pretty sure Mr. Swinehart will take over." He's been Mrs. Overstreet's assistant for four plays and would happily sell his grandmother for a shot at directing.

Dad puts down the newspaper and sips coffee.

"You wearing that?" He's eating cereal that comes in squares. But he's apparently paying more attention than I've given him credit for.

"Nope. I'm wearing what Mom has on." It's another lie, of course, and he laughs.

I may look thrown together, but this Bohemian, hippie-chic look has taken me all morning. I finally settled on a Language batik top—butterfly sleeves, naturally—over a Cultura long denim skirt. Sweet. Very sweet. I may or may not tie the bandana around my head when I get to school.

"When will Kyra's car be ready, Jeff?" Mom asks. She's eating half a bagel. But I know they have donuts waiting at the real-estate office.

"Next week at the earliest," Dad answers. "Sammy hasn't left yet, has he? You catching a ride with him, Kyra?"

"*Our* Sammy?" I ask. "No. He definitely hasn't left yet. And I'm not waiting on him."

What our parents don't know is that Sammy has had more tardies, and has talked his way out of more tardies, than any Macon High student. I think it will go in the record books, along with Manny's 99-yard touchdown and Jamal's high score of 57 points against Pearson High. It's like my brother is so good teachers can't believe he'd be late to their classes.

"How are you getting to school?" Mom asks, glancing at the clock above the stove. "You're going this early? Maybe I can take you if–"

"Thanks." Seniors don't get driven anywhere by their mothers, except maybe crazy. "I'm going with

Dylan. We're stopping by the hospital to see Bethany. She's in for a bunch of blood work."

"Say hello for us," Mom says, slipping into her suede jacket and hooking her arm through her purse. "You should bring her something, Kyra." She runs to her "gift closet" and comes back with a cute stuffed penguin. Mom is like her own store, picking up things she knows she'll need one day and storing them in the closet.

"So—" Mom takes a last sip of coffee and puts the mug in the dishwasher—"everything's going well at school then?"

No. Everything is not well. I feel like I'm losing my A in French. D.J.'s bugging me to go out with him every night. And I can't get my mind off that little orange bottle you hide in the medicine cabinet behind the calamine lotion.

"All is well," I say.

She kisses the top of my head and dashes out.

Dylan's waiting in his car, the motor running. When I get in, I glimpse the backseat. He must have worked hard to clean up the blood. I still smell blood mixed with ammonia and Old Spice.

At the hospital we have only a few minutes with Bethie, who loves her penguin. She has charmed the entire hospital staff. It's a small hospital, but everybody says we're lucky to have one at all in Macon.

"So, Bethie," I say, sitting on the foot of her bed, "if your house is on fire and you can only take three things, what would you take?"

She giggles. It's a game we've played forever. Even Dylan and I used to play.

"Um . . . hot dogs . . ." Her face squeezes together in concentration. "My smell jars . . ." Bethie collects smells in little jars and bottles—everything from fresh-baked chocolate-chip-cookie smell to her new bike to a thunderstorm. She just opens the bottles and captures the smell and never removes the lids again. So who knows? Maybe the smells take root in Bethany's bottles and last forever. "And Penguin!" she concludes, hugging her gift.

Dylan and I kiss Bethie good-bye and race back to the car before we're late for class.

Dylan's pulling out of the parking lot when he asks, "So what did you leave?"

I check my backpack, thinking he means I left it in the hospital. But it's on the backseat. I didn't take it in. "What?"

"I saw you take the pencil when we signed in. I just figured you left something, too."

"I took the pencil?" I resist the urge to stick my hand into my left coat pocket, where the purloined pencil lies.

Dylan groans. "This is Dylan, Kyra. Not your parents."

I don't say anything. What's there to say to that one?

We hit a red light, and he stops, then turns, waiting. "You still playing Robin Hood?"

I am beyond embarrassed. I forget how well this guy used to know me. Other than Sammy, Dylan is the only non-supernatural being who knows about this.

For as long as I can remember, I've picked up little things from one place and returned them to someplace else. I don't know when I started, but I did it with crayons in kindergarten—hanging on to

Alison's blue, then dropping it in Zach's box, taking Zach's green and giving it to Melissa. People don't even notice things like that.

Dylan caught on the first summer our families vacationed together. We stayed in a cabin on Lake Geneva. Dylan and Sammy and I had such a great time. Every morning we counted down the days we had left. On the last day, as we loaded the car, I wanted to leave something, a part of me, in the cabin. I scratched the windowsill in the bathroom, just with my fingernail, and imagined that scratch still there when I'd bring my own kids on vacation years in the future. Then I left my nickel—Dylan's dad had given us both one—in the drawer by my bed.

But Dylan found it and brought it out to the car for me. Earlier that day he'd caught me pocketing a screw that had kept coming out of the sink cabinet. So when I grabbed the returned nickel and ran back inside the cabin to put it back in the bedside drawer, Dylan figured everything out. He called me Robin Hood for a year after that.

"It was a fair exchange, Little John," I say, doing my best to make a joke out of it. "D.J.'s pen for a hospital pencil."

I can't tell if Dylan disapproves, which was always a nice thing about having him as a buddy. I could do things I knew he'd never do in a million years, but it never felt like he was judging me.

"How about you?" I ask, reinforcing the joke aspect of these revelations. "Are you still writing anonymously to single women?"

Dylan breaks out into a real laugh, total and sincere. I could bottle his laugh. Start my own collection. "I haven't thought about that one in a long time. When was that, junior high?"

When we were kids, Dylan used to send thank-you cards to total strangers. He'd get the names out of the phone book, picking the first names that were just initials because they were the most likely to be single women, maybe with kids they were struggling to raise on their own. He'd sign the card: "From all of us, for all you do. We appreciate you!" I think he spent half his allowance on cards.

Dylan takes the back way, avoiding Main Street and school buses. We skirt McCray's farm.

"Is the McCray pond still there?" I ask, pointing out the window. It's too dark to see much. "I haven't been out there for years." Dylan and I used to fish there when we were kids. Sammy, too.

It must be memory lane we're driving on. Maybe it's because it's Dylan, and our friendship, or relationship, now ekes by on bits of our regurgitated past.

"That pond is more like a lake these days," Dylan says. "I took Bethany fishing there a couple of times last summer. Did you know Mr. McCray died?"

I shake my head. I know I should say, "No! How did he die?" But I don't want to know. And if we move on, I can probably keep thinking of him out in the field, plowing. "Catch any fish?"

"A few. Bethie caught two. Mrs. McCray leaves the rowboat out all year and lets us take it whenever we want."

Sometimes when I'm with Dylan, I feel 10 years old. In a good way. And all I want to do is go fishing with him.

We park in the senior lot and walk in together.

"Need a ride after school?" Dylan asks. "Maybe we could get ice cream. Take some back to Bethie?"

"Thanks, Dylan. Wish I could." We step into packed halls. Lockers slam in off-beat, tinny percussion. I raise my voice. "Cheerleading practice."

Dylan nods. He's already moving down the hall to his class. For some reason I watch him, surprised that he's taller than most of the kids he passes.

"Kyra!" Miranda jog-walks toward me, her books precariously balanced in her arms. She tries to wave, but her hands are full and she nearly stumbles. Instead of the boots she had on yesterday, she's got her black tennis shoes, making her size-11 foot look more like Sammy's 13.

I wave. I think I'm glad to see her. We've known each other since kindergarten, when Sammy and I both hooked up with her. Since then I guess we've gone up and down. But we've been pretty tight for a year or so. "Miranda!" I shout. "Didn't we already have a heart-to-heart about those shoes?"

"Shelby *borrowed* my bootlaces last night!" she shouts back.

I don't ask why she didn't reclaim the laces this morning. They're probably not back yet.

I head for first period, which Miranda has, too. She does an about-face and falls in next to me. "How was NYU?"

"Great!" Certain things *were* great.

Usually, unless I'm ducking D.J. or somebody,
I hang in the hall until last bell. Wouldn't want to
miss anything. But today I want to get to class early.
I want a front-row seat for the Mitch Wade Show,
and they're not easy to come by.

Miranda and I make our entrance but stop in the
doorway. Apparently we're not the only ones buck-
ing for the expensive seats in Mitch's ballpark. Every
desk in the first two rows is filled. Tressa, short skirt,
legs crossed, has front-row center.

"Tried to save you a seat, Kyra!" she calls, then
shrugs.

Right.

Miranda and I join the last-row people in the
bleacher seats.

"Do you think—" Miranda starts. But then *he*
appears.

We all stop talking and watch as he closes the
door and sits on his desk, staring back at us. "I want
us to talk about something today," he says, as if we're
the only people on earth who matter, the only ones
he'd count on with whatever he wants to discuss.

"So . . . what are you saying?" Tony asks, pulling
out his lit book. "Another class discussion? Aren't
we ever going to get to our text in this class? Some
of us have freshman English in universities in a few
months." He opens his lit book. "Maybe we need to
know—"

Mitch crosses the room and snatches the book out
of Tony's hands. When he slams it shut, the thump
echoes. "We are going to learn more from life than
from books this semester, Tony."

Tony hasn't moved. His hands still hold an invisible book.

"I love that!" Yvonne cries.

"I'm in no rush for any schoolbook, man," Manny says.

"Good." Mitch eyes us. I think he rests his gaze on Miranda and me a little longer than anywhere else. "What is beauty? Someone define it for me."

Chairs squeak. Whispers spark up around the room.

"Come on. Anybody?"

Brianna stands up, turns around, and bows.

We laugh.

"At least now we know what modesty is *not,*" Rebecca mutters.

"Okay." Mitch drags his chair closer to us. "Let's try this another way. *Time* magazine surveyed men across the United States and asked them what's the first thing they notice about women. Ninety-five percent of them answered 'the eyes.' What does that tell you?"

"That 95 percent of men are liars?" I suggest.

The class cracks up.

"All right. Maybe not the best example. Let's go back to Brianna."

Brianna squirms in her seat.

"We might all agree that Brianna is beautiful."

It's debatable, but I let it go. The girl is suffering enough.

"We might all agree that Tressa is beautiful."

"Wow! Thanks, Mitch!" Tressa exclaims.

He ignores her. "But we might not agree which one is more beautiful."

Tressa and Brianna exchange frowns.

"So," Mitch continues, "does that make some of us wrong and others right?"

"No," Melissa answers. "It's just your opinion."

"Exactly!" Mitch stands up. "It's opinion. And it's relative. People in Kenya may think they're both ugly."

"Hey!" Brianna objects.

"Ask me," Jamal throws in, "we got us a roomful of dimes right here."

Mitch looks confused.

"Dimes? As in *10*s, females who score 10 on a Neanderthal's *chick* scale," I explain.

Dave eyes the class. "I agree. There's a roll of dimes in here."

"And a few guys who're about a nickel short of a dime," I add.

Everybody laughs. I was kind of with Tony in the beginning, about Mitch's needing to get on the ball and prep us for college classes. The NYU visit made me want to be as prepared as I could before I go there. But Mitch's discussions are proving to be the best.

"What about colors?" Mitch asks. "A few years ago, nobody would have sold a purple car. Now they're everywhere. Men only wore white shirts, never earrings. Look at the old high school pictures lining our halls, Class of '38, '49, '56, '77. We laugh at the way they're dressed, their hairstyles. But what makes our perception better than theirs? Nothing! And in a few years, students at this school will be laughing at *your* senior pictures." He lets that sink in before going on. "I like classical and jazz, but you like rock and R & B. So what? It's opinion, and it's relative."

He's making sense. But I'm not sure where he's going with it.

"So what if I don't think it's right to kiss on the first date, but you do?"

"Then you don't have as much fun as me," Dave says.

Mitch laughs with us. "Think about it. What if you do something I think is wrong, but you think's okay?"

The white pill pops into my head. I can see myself floating in the swimming pool. I'd felt lousy on the flight back Sunday, partly sick and partly feeling guilty.

"Who's to say my morals are better than yours, as long as you don't hurt anybody?" Mitch reasons.

We're silent for a minute. I try to look into kids' faces to see what they're thinking. Zach's asleep. Jenna looks like she doesn't get it. Tyrone's sneering like he knows something the rest of us don't. Miranda's hanging on every word. And I'm thinking maybe it wasn't so wrong to take that pill. It didn't hurt anybody.

Taylor raises her hand. She's at least as pretty as Brianna and way nicer. "There's a difference between opinions and morals and facts, though."

"Tell me the difference," Mitch says, his voice even.

"If we make up our own morals, then I suppose you're right. But if we get our morals from God, the facts in the Bible, then right and wrong have a factual basis. They're not opinions."

Mitch smiles at her, like she's younger than the rest of us. "Right and wrong," he repeats. You can tell he thinks he has her. Mitch is so logical, so real. I feel sorry for Taylor. She's out on a limb by herself. "What if I don't believe in *your* God, in *your* particular right and wrong?"

Taylor doesn't flinch. She returns Mitch's smile. "Facts are true whether you believe them or not, aren't they? You might not believe there's an Empire State Building, but it doesn't mean the building doesn't exist."

Other kids chime in on both sides. I listen to the discussion grow in volume and pitch. But I've stopped paying attention. I'm tired, so tired of *dreading one day at a time.* And besides, I've heard all I need.

I get a ride home from a cheerleading mom after practice. As I fish out my key, I glance around. Our garage door is down, and there's no sign of life inside my house.

Once inside, I chuck my bookbag on the floor and check the garage to make sure they're all gone. Then I yell upstairs to be double sure. "Hello! Anybody home?"

No answer.

I tiptoe up the stairs, even though I know nobody's around to hear me. At the top I keep going straight, to Mom and Dad's bedroom. The bed is made, no wrinkles. I don't have to lift the flowered bedspread to know that underneath lie flowered sheets with hospital corners.

Their wedding picture sits framed on the big

dresser. I can see Sammy in Dad's grin and the way he's standing. I can't see myself in either of my parents. Mom's auburn hair is short, clinging to her oval face. She's thin, with a waist that would please Scarlett O'Hara. But she looks nervous and out of place, like she's surprised to be included in the wedding photo.

I have to hurry. Mom could come home any minute. So could Sammy.

I keep moving through the bedroom to the half-bath, which I've always thought was a stupid thing to call a bathroom just because it doesn't have a tub. There are virtually no mirrors in this room, just a small, decorative mirror glass on the medicine cabinet door above the sink.

I see myself in it. It stops me for an instant, as if I've been caught, nailed, found out. But I reach up and open the cabinet. Then I can't see my reflection any longer, only three shelves of ointments, toothpaste . . . and pills.

I know which bottle to reach for, right behind the calamine.

I line up the arrows on the cap and flip it off. My fingers reach inside and pull out one white oval pill. One. Scored, creased down the middle in a perfect, straight line, as if anybody who would take one would take half—save the rest for later.

Right.

I drop it onto the back of my tongue and swallow, not waiting for a glass of water to wash it down. With one motion, I snap the lid back on and place the bottle back in the same spot, behind the pink bottle of calamine lotion. Then I shut the cabinet, being careful not to look in the little mirror.

■ ■ ■

For the next several days, I take one white pill every day—always and only one. I'm no addict. It's not even a habit formed. One night, when Mom took the afternoon off, I didn't even take a Zanax.

Mom never notices that her pills are going down faster. I don't care if they run out. She'll get more. Besides, they're not working like they did in New York. Each time I take one, the good feeling seems weaker, and it never lasts as long. Maybe if Mom runs out of pills, she'll get us some better ones.

■ ■ ■

Toward the end of January, I start to wonder if we'll even have a senior play. Part of me would resent not having one, but part of me would feel relieved. I don't know which *part* is real and which is false. Will the real Kyra please stand up?

Then one day, when Miranda and I have resigned ourselves to seats in the back of English class, Mitch walks in with a battered bag—leather, black, and big enough to hold a basketball. He plops the bag on his desk and turns to us exactly as the last bell rings.

"Shakespeare." He says it like D.J. might say fudge brownie.

Someone, I think Tressa, groans.

It is Tressa because Mitch turns to her and narrows

his eyes. "I might groan with you over half of the so-called literary greats. But Shakespeare is different. He's the real deal."

"But he's so hard to understand," Tressa moans.

"I'll read that there Shakespeare junk," Hale Ramsey drawls, "as long as one of y'all comes along afterwards and tells me what I done read."

I know this is bull. Hale wouldn't read Shakespeare if the old guy had written the secret to four-wheel drive. Hale is a hillbilly, and he hangs out with Tyrone. Both of them came to Macon our freshman year. Rumor has it that Hale spent time in a juvenile detention center somewhere in Kentucky before Iowa inherited him.

"Shakespeare doesn't need explaining! To explain is to ruin!" Mitch gestures with both hands in the air. Any other teacher who tried to get us to take school this seriously would get laughed off his desk.

But we're hanging on words, waiting for more to fall, clutching at them when they do.

"Shakespeare doesn't explain his characters. He sets them in motion. He lets them go. He doesn't care if we like them or if they like each other. He just wants to sit back and watch these fascinating people who can't be predicted or explained." Mitch sits on his desk, ankles crossed. "'All the world's a stage, And all the men and women merely players.'"

The room is quiet. And I'm thinking that Shakespeare must have known me in another life.

Mitch opens his bag and takes out a stack of paper books. They smack the desk when he sets them down. He turns back to us. "*As You Like It.*

It's an amazing play, filled with passion, love, loss, intrigue, comedy . . . life."

My head starts throbbing. *As You Like It*. Shakespeare. The *books* on his desk are scripts.

Our senior play is on. But it's not Mr. Swinehart who'll direct it. Not Mrs. Overstreet's assistant, who already knows what I can do. *He's* the new director. Mitchell Wade. Mitch. The teacher who can't decide if I'm invisible or someone who dreads every day, one at a time.

"Are you directing the senior play?" Brianna asks, voicing my nightmare.

Mitch pats the stack of scripts and smiles. *"As You Like It."*

"I like it," Brianna mutters.

Several kids chuckle.

Miranda's staring at me, and I know I have to get it together. It's just that everybody knows me except this new guy. I don't like starting over with people.

"And I want you all to try out," Mitch says. "It will be fun."

"You want us *all* to try out?" Tressa asks. She turns in her chair to look at me.

"All of you who want to," Mitch clarifies.

"Our reigning drama queen, Kyra James, has taken the lead every year since kindergarten," Jamal informs him. He turns and winks at me. "She's going to NYC next year to actress school."

There. Thank you, Jamal.

"That's fine," Mitch says, getting to his feet. "But I think we'll still hold official tryouts, if that's all right with you."

I manage to grin at the kids who glance back
at me to see what I'll do with this. This includes
Sammy, who hasn't acted since our commercial
days. He winks at me. He never could read me like
I read him.

Pain arcs from one temple to the other as if
someone's electrocuting my head for crimes against
the state. I need to calm down. I know I can act.
And I know I'll put more into the tryout than anyone in the school. I'll memorize the lines. Some kids
just read them onstage for auditions. I'll practice at
home more than anybody. It will turn out right.

Mitch stands up and takes his stack of scripts
and starts passing them out.

I lean back in my chair, relieved. If I have a copy
of the actual script, I can start memorizing right
after cheerleading practice.

He hands Miranda one, then me.

"Which lines do you want us to read for Rosalind's part?" I ask, leafing through the script. I know
the play. I read both of Mrs. Overstreet's possible
choices. Rosalind is the lead.

He doesn't answer right away. Instead he finishes
passing out the scripts, then takes the front of the
room again. "So that we're all in the same boat,
sinking and swimming together," he says, "I'm not
giving you any time to prepare. I want you to read
for your parts . . . right now."

"We can't try out now!" I protest. "We haven't
even seen the scripts." I try to soften it with a
chuckle.

"You haven't read the play, Kyra?" Mitch asks,

squinting at me as if he knows better. "That surprises me."

"I haven't read *this* script." I place my hand on it as if I'm being sworn in for the jury.

Mitch lets it drop. "I don't want to summarize the play." He's moving around in front of us, talking to the class now. My interview with Mitch is over. "Wouldn't dare ruin a Shakespeare masterpiece for you."

Hale groans.

"But what I want you to feel is that all the world is a stage. Think of it! When this play ran, in Shakespeare's day, all the actors were male."

"Sweet!" Tressa exclaims. "So just the guys can try out, right?"

"I want to see Manny play one of the girl parts!" Brianna shouts. "Great legs!"

I try to laugh along with them. But what I want to do is run to the bathroom and hurl. I can't do this. I can't try out, not without working the lines first.

Mitch continues as if he hasn't been interrupted. "Yet in the play, the character, Rosalind, will pretend she's a boy. So it's a boy pretending to be a girl pretending to be a boy. Why? So that she can teach the one she loves all about love. Don't you see? It's brilliant!"

A few of the kids—Tony, Luke, Amanda—nod appreciatively.

"Rosalind isn't the only good female part though," Mitch assures us. "There's the beautiful Celia—"

"Perfect for Manny!" Brianna exclaims.

Manny throws his pen at her. It misses and rolls to my feet.

I pick it up and don't give it back.

Mitch laughs. "For the readings, we'll be working from one of Rosalind's speeches—girls only; sorry, Manny—and the famous speech of Jaques, one of the lords attending Duke Senior."

"I don't want to do this," Miranda whispers.

I take a deep breath and force myself casual. My scalp feels tight, like it doesn't fit any longer and might snap off my head. "Why can't we take the scripts home and do the readings tomorrow?" I ask.

"Because we can't," he answers. "Sometimes there are no reasons and no answers."

I would like to throw my script at him and walk out the door.

"Okay then!" Mitch bounds to the desk and picks up his copy of *As You Like It*. He turns pages, then folds the book back and holds it in one hand. "Turn to page 41, the long speech by Jaques."

I glance at the clock. He's starting with the boys. He won't have time for Rosalind's part, not this hour. And if he does get to the females, he'll probably choose me last again anyway. I don't need to worry like this. But I can't seem to stop.

"Brent." Mitch is starting with our benchwarmer, which might be funny under different circumstances. But nothing feels funny now.

"Me?" Brent, who's been slouching, his back nearly on the seat of his chair, pulls up straight. "I've never been in a play."

I can't help grinning, at least inside. Mitch isn't

as smart as he thinks he is. Brent's a fatal first choice.

"Great!" Mitch declares. "Then nothing in your past should get in the way of your becoming this character. I'll start you off with the short speech by Duke Senior just before your cue. Got it?"

Brent folds his script like Mitch's and clears his throat.

The room is as silent as opening night.

Mitch crosses the room to Brent and reads:

> *"Thou seest we are not all alone unhappy.*
> *This wide and universal theater*
> *Presents more woeful pageants than the*
> *   scene*
> *Wherein we play in."*

He's good. I think we all realize it. If you hadn't heard Mitch talk before, you'd swear he's a British citizen. He peers up from the script and fixes his gaze on Brent.

Even from where I'm sitting, two rows back, I see Brent's Adam's apple bob as he swallows and scoots up even straighter. His back hasn't been this rigid since he started warming the bench at games.

Brent begins reading so softly, I can barely hear him:

> *"All the world's a stage,*
> *And all the men and women merely*
> *   players.*
> *They have their exits and their entrances,*

And one man in his time plays many
parts,
His acts being seven ages. . . .

Brent gets louder with every line. We're silent
as snowfall, amazed at this reading, this reader. He's
coming off the bench and stepping up to the free-
throw line, talking about the parts we play in life,
as if he's thought of this for years and only now is
deciding to share it with the rest of the world.

"Last scene of all, that ends this strange
eventful history,
Is second childishness and mere oblivion,
Sans teeth, sans eyes, sans taste, sans
everything."

Nobody says a word. Only when Brent looks
up does he become Benchwarmer Brent again. His
cheeks flush, and his shoulders sag back in place.

Sammy claps first. Then we all do. And I think
we couldn't have been more surprised if Manny had
nailed a girl's reading.

Mitch doesn't heap praise on Brent, not with
words. But it's in his look, a conspiratorial *we-
showed-them-didn't-we-buddy* grin. He calls on three
more guys to read the same part. Jamal isn't half-
bad, but the others are.

Then Mitch shifts gears. "Who would like to try
out for Rosalind's role?"

My stomach hurts as much as my head. I can't
look. I don't want to see hands raised, not for a role

everybody until today had assumed was mine. Maybe I shouldn't have assumed it, but I did. And they did. Until *he* came.

"Great. Brianna?" Mitch smiles at her raised hand and then ferrets through the script.

I glare at the back of Brianna's head. There's no love lost between us. We've liked the same boys for most of high school, often at the same time.

"What page?" she asks, taking the gum out of her mouth. Who knows where she puts it? Her voice is breathy and low. Guys probably think it sounds sexy, but it's weak—too weak when she's cheering on the football field sidelines. And it's definitely not a stage voice.

Mitch tells her the page, and they read a scene, though it's hard to make it out because Brianna can't get through a whole line without cracking up. She laughs the words, laughs when Mitch says his lines seriously.

I'm not as mad at her as I was.

"Miranda, you give it a read," Mitch says, as if they're old acting partners and he wants her to show us how it's done.

"No thanks," she says, staring at the cover of *As You Like It*, as if there might be a door there she can escape through.

"It's just a reading. Doesn't mean anything. We'll schedule tryouts for next week or the week after. You won't even have to audition if you decide you don't want to be involved in the play." Desks scoot aside to make room for him as he passes through us, Moses to our Red Sea. He comes all the way back to

tower over Miranda in the back row. He's so close
I can smell suntan lotion. If I had a jar, I'd save the
smell for Bethie's collection.

Mitch squats down so Miranda has to look
straight at him. "Please? A short scene. You'll read
Rosalind, and I'll read Orlando." It's like he's forgotten the rest of us are out here. He finds the right
page for Miranda and points to her part. "You and
I are in love."

Guys should be hooting, saying crude jokes. But
they're not. They're turned in their seats, watching,
as if Miranda and Mitch are onstage.

Mitch keeps explaining to her. "You're pretending to be a young man, and you've offered to
give me advice on love, for I have fallen deeply
in love with Rosalind—you—though I don't know
it yet."

Then he starts, not waiting for Miranda to agree
to this:

> Mitch: "I swear to thee, youth, by the
>   white hand of Rosalind, I am that he,
>   that unfortunate he."
> Miranda: "But are you . . . are you . . . "

She glances up at Mitch, pleading to stop the
show, but he nods for her to go on.

> Miranda: "But are you so much in love as
>   your rhymes speak?"
> Mitch: "Neither rhyme nor reason can
>   express how much."

Miranda: *"Love is merely a madness and,
I tell you, deserves as well a dark house
and a whip as madmen do; and the
reason why they are not so punished and
cured is that the lunacy is so ordinary
that the whippers are in love too."*

"Yes!" Mitch hops up and spins around, returning to the front. "Well done!"

I manage to smile at Miranda. Mitch is right. "Great job, Miranda," I whisper.

She glances at me, as if she thinks I'm kidding, teasing her. Then she stares down at the script and twists a strand of her hair. "That was awful," she whispers. "I'm never doing that again."

But it wasn't awful. And Miranda is the only one who doesn't know that.

My chest feels tight, like I'm wearing a corset or armor, instead of this gauze blouse. I want the class to be over. I'll be okay again tomorrow. I'll be able to speak then, to breathe.

"Kyra." Mitch says it loud, as if it's the second or third time he's said it and I haven't heard. "Your turn. Page 55."

I glance at the clock again, willing the hands to move. For some reason, Dylan pops into my mind, and I wish he'd taken this class with me. I even wish I had *his* Jesus in here. And I think how stupid this is. Even I know Jesus has to be in here. But it's been so long since I've prayed. No way would God step in and calm me down now. Works for Dylan. Not me.

"It's the one I just read with Miranda," Mitch says, as I'm leafing through the pages, trying to see the numbers.

I can hear blood rushing through my ears, roaring, laughing.

Mitch reads the cue line. But I've lost it on the page. It's like the words are moving, the lines snaking so I can't read them.

He's quiet, waiting.

"Okay. I have it now," I say. I try to shut out the weird looks I'm getting. Jamal doesn't know whether to grin or not, like he thinks I'm doing this on purpose. Sammy looks like he's eaten a lemon.

Mitch reads the line again.

> Me: "But are you in . . . no, are so in love
> . . . wait a minute. Let me start again.
> But are you so much in love that your
> rhymes speak?"
> Mitch: "Neither rhyme nor reason can
> express how much."

It's my turn. I can see the line, read the "Rosalind." I try to say it. I think I do. But I can't hear myself because of the blood rushing through my ears. And I can't remember if I already read this line or not.

Mitch stops reading. I don't think we've finished the scene. I'm sure I didn't read as much as Miranda did. But he closes the script and walks to the other side of the room.

"How about it, Jenna? Want to give it a try?" Mitch asks.

Even Miranda isn't looking at me. Nobody is.

And if I can't stop the rush in my ears and the pounding in my brain, I'm afraid I'm going to scream.

I have never failed so miserably at anything, not in my entire life, not even in my nightmares.

I stay in my seat while the room empties. Kids plop down their scripts on the teacher's desk as they file out. My head has turned to steel, and it takes all my energy to keep my forehead from dropping onto the desk arm.

"Aren't you coming?" Miranda asks. She and I are the only students left in the room, although I can see Sammy waiting outside.

"In a minute. You go on."

She slides up the aisle, bumping a desk as she turns for the door.

Mitch is loading his leather bag and acting like he doesn't see me. At least I think he's acting. He's so good it's hard to tell.

I get up. My head feels like it stayed in the chair

longer than the rest of me and has to rush to catch up. "I want another try."

"Excuse me?" Mitch glances at me and then goes back to packing his stupid bag.

"Another read." I know he knows what I mean. He's making me ask, making me beg.

"Don't worry about it, Kyra." He snaps the bag shut. "Tryouts will be next week. This was just a read-through."

"I want another read-through then," I say, reaching his desk, stopping a foot from him, close enough to see that he has a black speck in the white of his eye.

"We really can't take more than two class days with the readings. And we didn't get very far today. It wouldn't be fair to let you do two."

"I can do it later then." I'm trying not to sound so needy. This isn't me talking, begging.

He narrows his eyes at me. "After you have a chance to study the lines?"

"Then I'll read now!"

"I have a class now. So do you, I imagine."

"After school then!" Let the cheerleaders cheer without *this* leader.

He whisks his leather bag off his desk, ready to walk out. "Can't. I promised some of the guys we'd bike after school."

"After that then?" He's making this so hard. I know he's doing it on purpose.

He takes a step toward the door, and I think he's going to leave me like this. Then he turns back. "Okay. Come by the bike shop. Just before closing. We'll do it then."

■ ■ ■

I don't see Sammy again until lunch. D.J. and I have been running options for Saturday night, and I've successfully steered him away from his top three movie picks.

Miranda hasn't said much or eaten much. But then I haven't even touched my taco. It sounded good until I set it on my tray. Then it smelled weird, like Mexican tanning oil. My stomach's too knotted to let anything in anyway.

"Yo, Sis!" Sammy balances his tray on his fingertips, waiter-style, as he sidles over to us. "What was up in Mitch's class?" He sits down next to me at the table, facing the wrong way.

I shrug. "Killer headache."

He bumps shoulders. "You okay now?"

"Yeah. You want my taco?"

He's clearly done eating and on his way to dump the trash. But he takes the taco. "Later!" he shouts as he weaves through the masses.

The cafeteria is so noisy I feel like I have to get out of here. When I stand up, I catch a glimpse of Tyrone Larson. He's sitting by himself a table over, but he's staring at me, and he doesn't bother to turn away when I catch him at it. Except for Hale, who seems to be around him constantly, Tyrone is a loner. He's the kind of guy who'd refuse to leave the building for a fire alarm because he doesn't trust electricity and he doesn't like crowds.

D.J. follows my X-ray vision to Tyrone, then

goes back to his burritos. "So maybe we'll go to a party or something."

I pull loose from the Tyrone-stare-down. "What did you say, D.J.?"

"Saturday. Like a party or something?"

"Yeah. Okay." I don't know where D.J. parties, but it's got to beat Vin Diesel. "Whatever."

■　　■　　■

The afternoon goes slower and slower, like it's winding down. A couple of kids from English ask me about my botched script reading. I give each of them a different answer, but I don't say I'm doing it over. I'm not sure why.

My do-over is all I can think about, though. I keep replaying the morning, the way I messed up in front of everybody, in front of Mitch. I know I need to chill, to relax, to get the edge off. And I can't do that without a little help.

Brianna and I have last-hour study hall together. I skip my usual spot by the magazines and drop my stuff at her table.

"Kyra!" she exclaims, in spite of the fact that last bell's rung and Ms. Bowers is yelling at us to be quiet.

I take the seat next to her, and she looks a little worried. Luke Perrier is at the table. He's another jock we've both dated. I give Luke my best smile, just to reinforce Brianna's worst fears. Actually, Luke's going with Amy Sing, who's a lot nicer than Brianna and me put together. Sammy dated her our sophomore year.

"Weren't we *awful* in Mitch's class!" Brianna laughs. Her sound is metallic and loud enough to hear over a nuclear holocaust.

Ms. Bowers gives us a dirty look.

"Yes, we were awful," I admit, inwardly objecting to her *we*. I'm not like her. I just had a bad morning. "Listen, I don't feel that hot. I'm going home right after this."

"But what about practice?"

"Tell everybody I've got a headache." I can't remember the last cheerleading practice I missed. But this is an emergency. "You guys don't need me anyway."

Brianna shrugs, as if who's she to argue with that.

■　■　■

As soon as study hall is over, I run to my locker, grab my stuff, and head for the parking lot. Dylan is already unlocking his car when I spot him.

"Dylan!" I wave until he waves back.

He leans on his car while I brave the pick-up lane and cross to the senior lot.

"Thought you had cheerleading practice," he says when I make it around the last car and jog up to him.

"Me too." Not a lie exactly. "Can you drop me home?"

"Hop in."

On the way home Dylan doesn't ask about my read-through with Mitch, although I'd bet my pom-poms he's heard all about it. He doesn't mention English class at all. I try to listen as he tells me about how Bethany's starting to read better on her own and that she loves reading her Bible.

But all I can think about is getting something to help calm me down. In a couple of hours, I'll be reading for Mitch again.

" . . . if you want to go sometime." Dylan glances at me, expecting me to say something.

"I'm sorry, Dylan. Headache. What did you say?"

He smiles without showing teeth. "It's okay. Here we are." He pulls into my driveway. "Let me know if you need a ride tomorrow."

"Thanks, Dylan." I get out and shut the door softly, but it makes my head vibrate. "I'll call you. Give Bethie a kiss for me!"

My hand won't hold still at the door as I fumble with the key in the lock. Finally I get it, and the door *whooshes* open. Quiet meets me in the entry. The clock ticks. The ice maker dumps cubes on other cubes.

"Anybody home?" I holler.

When nobody answers, I take the stairs two at a time and go straight to the medicine cabinet. The orange plastic bottle is right where I left it. My fingers squeeze and jerk at the lid until I remember to line up the arrows.

Then it pops.

I shake out one pill, clutch it, and put the bottle back, turning off lights as I leave the bedroom. The radio alarm clock reads 3:45.

It's early. The bike shop doesn't close until 5:30.

I should wait to take the pill until 5 so it's still work-ing when I need it.

I go to my room and set the pill on the end table next to my bed. It surprises me to see I haven't made my bed. I may be a slob in many ways—shirts and skirts on chairs, junk shoved into the closet, socks and bra on the floor—but I always make my bed.

I pull up the covers and set my study pillow against the headboard. My Shakespeare paperbacks are right where I left them, *As You Like It* next to *Taming of the Shrew* on the top shelf on my book-case. Taking *As You Like It* to bed and settling back against the study pillow, I leaf through the script. I should have enough time to read every Rosalind speech, in case Mitch gets tricky and makes me read from a different scene.

Scanning for the first Rosalind dialogue, I glance at the nightstand, where the pill still sits next to my alarm.

I read a few pages silently, but it's hard to keep the words in my head. I can't focus.

Maybe what I should do is take the pill now. I think if I did, if I just took it and got it over with, I could concentrate. I could memorize the Rosalind speech we read in class and study the other lines, too. It's almost four.

I hold off another minute or two. But I'm not doing anybody any good like this. My mind's skip-ping all over the place. I hear the house sigh and think about my parents' sigh language. Branches scratch my window. The bed creaks.

I take the pill. No water.

It's a while before I can feel anything. And I'm thinking, like I always do, that the pill isn't going to work this time. The thought crosses my mind that Mom's onto me. Dad, too. That they've gotten together and switched pills, replacing the good ones with fakes.

Then the familiar calm sweeps into the room, into the bed, into my head. Like a fall breeze it blows past me, taking off the ragged edges of the day.

I'm tired. So sleepy. But I can see now, feel now, how ridiculous it was to get so upset over this reading. So that's good. I did the right thing, taking the pill early.

I read through Rosalind's lines, but it doesn't seem to matter so much now. And my eyes want to shut down, to stop seeing and let myself feel. Feel better.

■   ■   ■

I wake up with a jerk. Shakespeare falls to the floor. It takes me a minute to remember where I am, what I'm doing, why it's still light outside.

Somebody's on the stairs.

I jump out of bed and turn my alarm clock so I can see the face. It's almost *5:30!* Mitch!

I dash out of my room just as Sammy reaches the top stair. He's wearing his biker pants and carrying his helmet.

"Sammy! I need a ride!" I'd planned to walk to the bike shop, but there's no time now. Mitch could leave before I get there.

Sammy groans. "When's your car going to be ready anyhow?"

"Sammy, please!" There's no question that I slept off any help the Zanax might have given me. It's as if I'd never taken the thing. Or worse. My stomach hurts now. If Sammy weren't here, if I weren't so late already, I'd take another Zanax. Forget about my self-inflicted one-a-day rule.

"All right." Sammy steps around me. "Just give me a minute to shower and—"

I take his arm and pull him down the stairs with me. "There's no time! I have to get to the bike shop."

"You're kidding," Sammy says, letting me drag him. At the bottom of the stairs, he grabs his jacket, which reminds me to grab my coat. "I was just there, at the bike shop. Mitch is awesome. A bunch of us biked to—"

"You can tell me in the car!" I say, cutting him off and running the rest of the way.

On the drive to the bike shop, Sammy details his bike ride with Mitch and the guys. "Mitch says we can bike right through the winter, as long as the roads aren't icy. He's pretty amazing, Kyra. Did you know he used to enter those Iron Man contests? Mitch thinks I've got a good shot at triathlons."

Even Sammy sounds like he's under Mitch's spell. "I think you're all crazy to bike in this weather," I observe. "What is it—some kind of big male-bonding ritual?"

Sammy either doesn't get my sarcasm or pretends not to. "Nope, Rebecca and Taylor biked, too. And Randi! She was awesome!"

My chest hurts, probably from my heart pounding so hard. *Randi.* Sammy still calls Miranda that. She had the best reading in class. And now she's biking with Mitch.

I keep checking the time. It's after 5:30, but I'm counting on Mitch not closing on time.

We're almost there before Sammy asks me why I have to get to the bike shop.

"School stuff," I say, hoping he'll let it go at that.

He doesn't. Sammy and I haven't been really close for a long time, but we're still twins. We have that connection. He's always known a lot more about me than our parents have. For a minute I'm afraid he's going to ask me about the pills.

"It's about the play, right?" he asks.

I'm relieved. But I don't feel like talking to Sammy about the play either. "Maybe. Come on, Sammy! Take that spot in front." I point to the perfect parking place, where someone's just pulling out. "And don't wait on me. I'll walk home."

"You're going to get Mitch to let you try reading again, right?" Sammy shakes his head. "I knew you wouldn't be okay with that."

"So I'm not okay with that. And you're a mind reader. Congratulations. Are you going to turn in there or what?"

Sammy pulls across traffic to get the parking space in front of the shop. The *CLOSED* sign is already hanging on the door, but I see lights.

"Thanks, Sammy! See you later." I hop out, hoping he won't try to tag along.

I don't hear him pull away, so I wave over my shoulder. Finally he backs out and takes off.

I cup my hands to the glass to stare inside the bike shop. Four or five guys are standing by a long row of bikes.

I knock on the glass door.

The guys turn and squint, but they don't come to the door. I recognize Brent, Dave, Tyrone, and Hale.

Rattling the door latch to make sure it's locked, I knock again . . . and again . . . until I see Mitch stride out from somewhere in the back of the store. He comes directly to the front and frowns at me through the glass. Then he pulls out a key and unlocks the door. A bell rings when it opens.

"So you're open," I say, grinning, making a joke. "Hey, guys!" I call over.

Brent and Dave are wearing bike pants like Sammy's. Tyrone and Hale have jeans on.

"You missed a great ride, Kyra!" Brent hollers.

"Now, you know how I feel about sweat, Brent." I'm pulling it off, keeping it light. If Mitch knew how I really feel inside, he'd give me the Academy Award right now, skip the reading, skip the tryouts, skip the play. I turn to him and lower my voice. "Sorry I'm a tad late."

Mitch frowns, like he's sorry he ever agreed to this. "Well, unless you want an audience of sweaty bikers, you're going to have to wait awhile." He's wearing biker pants, too, with a long-sleeved T, but no sweat. "You guys feel free to pull out any of the bikes you want. Check them out. Let me get Kyra squared away. She's giving me a hand, catching me up on theater protocol at Macon High."

Brent nods, like he was wondering what I was doing here, but now he understands.

I'm impressed with how easily Mitch lied. I follow him to the back of the shop, to a small, closed-in office. The window to the front has been broken out and covered with plywood. The musty room feels more like a closet.

"I've really got to get this window fixed," he says.

Now that I'm here, alone with Mitch, I feel twice as anxious as I did in class. I could kick myself for taking the Zanax too early. I can't remember a single line of Rosalind's speech.

"You okay to wait here, Kyra?" Mitch asks. He's staring at me.

I feel my throat close, daring any words to come out. "You know what," I begin, "maybe this wasn't such a hot idea." My voice is too breathy, like Brianna's.

Mitch doesn't move. When he's listening, watching, it's as if nobody exists except us.

"Seriously, I'm having a really bad day. My head's ready to split open." And I realize it's true, that my pre-Zanax headache has come back with a vengeance.

"You're so uptight, Kyra," Mitch says softly.

I start to protest, to make a joke of it. But I stop. And I feel like I might cry if I don't get a grip on things. "I can't help it," I admit.

The teacher thing to do would be to tell me to talk to my parents or to the guidance counselor. Or to try to talk me out of it, to give me all the reasons why I of all people shouldn't be anxious about anything.

But Mitch doesn't do any of these things. "I hear that." He rubs the back of his neck. "I'm already feeling the Macon mania." He crosses to a gray metal desk that takes up one wall. "I got calls from the principal *and* the superintendent today." He opens the drawer and feels around inside. "Can you believe they want to know what I'm having my students read? In every class? They want a syllabus, too!"

I don't know what to say. I've never had a teacher talk to me like this. I don't know what I'm supposed to say.

"And doctors!" He's leaning down to see inside

the drawer. "Aren't there any *real* doctors in this town? I don't know where I'm going to get prescriptions anymore. They act like you need sworn testimony to give you an antibiotic."

I laugh a little. "Mom goes to Clarinda." It's a dumb thing to say. All I'd have to add is, *And that's where she gets the Zanax that aren't still working for me, so I can't do this reading.*

"Thanks. I'll try there."

Nothing about him is predictable.

"There!" He pulls a tiny glass bottle from his desk, opens it, shakes something into his hand, and sets the bottle on his desk. A bottle of Spring Water, half full, sits on the edge of his desk, and he uses it to swallow whatever he's got in his palm. He sets the water down hard enough to make a *twang* on the metal desk. "Better." He inhales deeply, exhales. "Much better." Mitch turns to me. "Sometimes you just need a little help."

I watch him walk to the office door. He opens it, then says over his shoulder, "Give me 10 minutes to get rid of these guys. Then we'll do that reading. Script's on my desk."

The little office feels like the air left with Mitch. I'm thirsty. And something's gnawing in my stomach.

The script. I walk over to the desk and see *As You Like It* lying next to the tiny bottle. I pick it up—the script—and find Rosalind's speech right off. But my eyes keep wandering to the glass bottle. It looks like it has a pharmacy label on it.

I sit on the desk and lean over to read the label: *Mitchell Wade . . . OxyContin.*

I'm disappointed. For a fleeting instant, I thought it might be Zanax, that maybe it would be all right to borrow one, replace it later, and get some help calming down for this reading. I know in my head how stupid it was to imagine Mitch just *happened* to be taking the same drug as my mom.

But the way he said *Better. Much better . . .* and the bit about needing a little help . . .

OxyContin, though, sounds like a laundry detergent.

I try to focus on Rosalind's speech, the one we did in class. But it only makes me more nervous. After a couple of tries through, whispering the words, I give up. No way I can do this now.

I slide off the desk and toss the script back. Then I leave the office. Brent and an older guy are the only ones left out front with Mitch.

"Could I see you for a second?" I ask.

Mitch says something to the guys and comes over. "Sorry. Maybe five more minutes, Kyra." He's inches from me.

"I'm sorry. I can't do it. My head . . . I don't know what's wrong."

Mitch lowers his voice. "I think you *should* do it, Kyra. If you don't, it might become a mental block. And we're holding tryouts next week." He glances at the guys, then fixes me with a stare that feels as though he can see through to my veins and arteries. "Sometimes people need a little help. It's that simple. Go back to my office, to my desk. Do what you need to do. And wait. I'll be right there. Okay?"

He's gone before I can say okay or not okay. I

watch him walk back to the others, while I try to keep the words with me. I'm not sure I heard him right.

Turning back, I enter the office and close the door. When I glance at the desk, the only thing I see is the glass bottle, as if it's grown while I was away.

It's that simple.

Did he mean *this?* This bottle?

No way.

No way he was telling me to go take one of his Oxy pills. I don't even know what they're for. They could be for sunburn for all I know.

But he left the bottle out. He sent me back to his desk. He said to do what I need to do.

I pick up the bottle and read the label again. The tablets are orange. I take off the lid and shake one into my hand. It's not scored, no groove down the center of this pill.

Sometimes people need a little help.

Before I can change my mind, I tilt my head back, place the pill on the back of my tongue, and swallow.

I have no idea how much time has passed when Mitchell Wade joins me in his office.

And I don't care.

"Sorry that took so long," he says. "Want to do that read-through now?"

"Absolutely!" I'm surprised how loud my voice sounds. But I don't care. I snatch the script off the desk and try to find the right page.

"Um . . . let me give you a hand with that." Mitch takes the script, folds it over, and hands back.

The words jump off the page, as if printed in bold. I can't wait to be . . . the character . . . whatever her name is. I feel I can nail this part, say it by heart, though I can't remember the lines or her name exactly. "Go!" I say. "I'll be . . . that girl . . . "

"Rosalind," Mitch says, completing my thought.

He reads some lines, but he's not reading. So I know he already has them memorized. And I admire him so deeply for that, I think I could cry.

But I'm too psyched. I read the next lines and keep going, maybe getting into Orlando's speech— I'm not sure. The words are flowing fast, and I don't want to stop them.

Mitch grins when I get to the end of the page.

"I nailed it, right?" I say, grinning back. My head is so clear. But I can't quite remember the character's name again. "Her part. I read it."

"Yes, you did, Kyra." He's still grinning.

"Was Miranda better?"

"Of course not."

"All right then." I get up, and for a minute, the room tilts and then centers again. I shake my head, and it does funny things to the little room.

Mitch walks to the door and then turns back to me. "Maybe you want to stay here for a while? How are you getting home?"

I picture Sammy pulling out of the parking space. "Walking." And suddenly walking sounds wonderful. "I'm going to walk!"

"That's probably a good idea. Why don't you hang around and go over the rest of the script before you take off?" Mitch leaves me in his office.

After a while—I'm not sure how long—Mitch comes back. "How are you feeling, Kyra? I need to get home. You okay?"

"I'm great!" I declare. The script is in my hand. I'm not sure if I've been reading it, or if I dozed off. When I stand up, the room doesn't sway though.

I start to follow Mitch out. Then I race back to the desk, pull Manny's pen out of my pocket, and drop it onto the desk. It doesn't seem like enough, so I untie the bandana from my head and shove it into the desk drawer and run outside.

It's surprisingly dark out, with a half-moon already higher than the Tiger Den's roof. The crisp night air freezes my eyeballs until I remember to blink.

"See you tomorrow!" Mitch calls. He unlocks his Porsche and climbs in. Then he drives off, leaving stillness behind him.

■ ■ ■

By the time I walk up the sidewalk to my house, my ears are numb, but I've stopped floating. I remember enough to know that whatever was in that Oxy pill is better than my mom's pills. I can almost see why people get addicted to drugs, although I never would. But it helped me through the reading, and that's enough. All I need.

Someone's knocking on the window next door, and I turn to see Bethany, lit up by her bedroom light on the second floor. I wave to her and think she looks more like an angel than ever. She picks up their dog, a dog-pound-rescued mutt, and makes him wave his paw at me.

Then just as suddenly as I'd gotten a charge of every positive feeling back in the bike shop, a wave of sadness slaps me down so hard I stumble on the curb. Not sadness for Bethany, but for me. I blow her a kiss and dash into the house.

The house smells like hot dogs, but I know Mom wouldn't have cooked hot dogs. Still, the odor is everywhere, and it makes me want to hurl.

"Kyra? Is that you?" Dad calls from the family room.

"Hi, Dad!" I call back. My voice sounds hoarse. "I've got a ton of homework!" I keep moving toward the stairs.

"Aren't you having dinner?" Mom shouts.

"I already ate. Thanks!" I hold the banister and take the stairs as fast as I can.

Sammy opens his door and sticks his head out. "Where've you been?"

"Bike shop."

"You're kidding." He glances at his watch. "All that time?"

I haven't looked at my watch, so I don't know how much time. But it's none of Sammy's business. "Back off. What are you, my keeper?"

His head snaps back as if I've cuffed him on the chin.

I round the landing and keep going to my room. I hear Sammy's door shut, and I slam mine, not sure why I'm so angry with him. It feels to me like he's done something to tick me off, but I can't remember what.

And I don't want to.

My neck feels stiff, and when I turn it, a sharp pain stabs from my hairline to my shoulder. I just want to sleep before I feel worse. But I have homework. I didn't finish my econ, and we're having a history quiz tomorrow, and something else, but I can't think what it is.

And I don't want to.

I kick off my ankle boots and see that my stockings are wet. My feet are frozen.

I haven't turned on the lights in my room, but through my window I see the glow of the Grays' roaring fireplace and smoke rising from their chimney. Shivering, I plop down on my bed, wrap the covers around me, and close my eyes.

■ ■ ■

When I open my eyes, I'm scared. For a second I don't know where I am, why I'm dressed, why it's light outside, why someone is beating down my door.

"Kyra! You better get up if you're riding with me!" Sammy is yelling on the other side of the door, my bedroom door.

"Yeah! I'm coming!" I turn the alarm and can't believe I have to leave for school in 15 minutes. I've slept all night. In my clothes. My mouth feels like desert rats have made it their home.

I get up too fast and have to sit back down. My head hurts, and my stomach feels empty. I have to get ready. Grabbing the nearest clothes I can find—the long denim skirt and a pullover sweater—I race to the bathroom. Sammy's finished with it, but there's still no time for me to shower. My hair looks so greasy that I decide to braid it. I splash water on my face and catch a glimpse of myself in the mirror. My eyes are puffy, and I look horrible without makeup.

"Kyra! I'm going in five minutes, with or without you!" Sammy yells.

That's it. I'm done with pills. The girl in the mirror is so not me.

I can't even remember what I felt like last night. But I feel so lousy now that I mean it. I'm done. Mom can keep her Zanax, and Mitch can have his Oxys. I can't even believe I took one of his pills or that I thought he meant for me to take it. I can't imagine facing him in class. What if he counts the pills and knows that I had one?

I tear down the stairs and dash out the door just as Sammy opens it. "You look . . . interesting."

"An actress has to keep trying new personae!" I shout back at him, wishing I'd taken my long coat instead of this bomber jacket. But at least I've got my wits back. And I can go over my history notes during lunch and fake econ until I can make up the assignment.

Kyra James will pull it off.

■　　■　　■

Miranda is waiting for me in English, her long legs stretched over the empty seat she's managed to save for me in the front row.

"Thanks." I drop my bookbag and slide into the seat as she retracts her legs. I've been feeling self-conscious about how sloppy I look . . . until I check out Miranda's outfit—black sweats and a T-shirt that says "Harry's Place" in silver letters. I won't even ask where the shirt came from. No doubt from one of Shelby's favorite bars.

"Braids?" Miranda asks, lifting one of my pigtails. Hairs are already escaping.

"I know."

"Hey!" Miranda leans closer and lowers her voice. "Ryan says you and D.J. are going to Eric's Saturday!"

Ryan is Ryan Emerson, Miranda's latest. He's not as cute as D.J., but close.

"We are?" I ask, pulling my history book out and turning to the quiz chapter. I managed to glance over my notes in the car by totally ignoring Sammy's questions until he gave up and turned on the radio. "Who's Eric?"

"D.J.'s brother. He graduated the year before last. Ryan and I are going. I guess he throws pretty cool parties."

I glance at Miranda. She's told me that all she wants to do her last semester of high school is to have some fun for a change. I didn't think she was serious, but maybe she is. She deserves some fun if anybody does. Her mother is 10 times wilder than Miranda.

"Cool. Who else is going?"

"I'm trying to get Alisha to go. Maybe fix her up with Jamal."

Mitch comes in, and it's like a spell falls over the room. I have to put my history book away because I'm right there in the front row, but I don't think I could have managed in the back row either.

"It's been a few years since I was your age."
Mitch offers his zillion-dollar variety smile. Age is
so overrated. "Are you seniors still as stressed as we
were?"

"More stressed, man!" Jamal declares.

"You got that right!" Tressa shouts. "We get it
from everywhere!"

"Like?" Mitch waits for details.

"Like Coach!" Manny puts in.

The jocks second Manny or groan with him.

"Big deal!" Brianna says. "Coach is the least
of my stress. *Guys* are stress!"

"You go, girl!" someone hollers.

"Parents!"

"Teachers!"

We laugh. I do, too. But I'm thinking they're
right, all of them. And I feel every stress they come
up with.

"Kyra?" Mitch stands in front of me.

Part of me wants to get serious, to tell everybody
in this room, especially Mitch, that I can hardly
handle the stress, that I've had *help*, pills, that I've
sworn off of them, but I can't stop thinking about
them.

But I can't do that.

"Hey, stress is all-American, right?" I say, already
getting a chuckle from Miranda. "Where else would
we have *Quick Stops*, Fast Lanes, Speedos–" That
one gets a roomful of laughs. "–*Day Runners* for
calendars, *Sprint* for phones, *Slim-FAST* if you want
to lose weight? We've even got a monument to
stress–Mount Rushmore!"

Everybody's cracking up . . . except Mitch.

"Does everybody agree we're forced into stress?" Mitch asks, as if this is big news to him.

Taylor raises her hand from the second row. Miranda glances over at her. They're pretty good friends, I think. Taylor is a girl jock, like Rebecca, only a lot nicer. She waits until Mitch nods for her to speak. "I don't think we can argue with the fast pace of life. There's a lot of stress out there. But we still have choices. We can choose what we want to do and what we don't want to do."

"Choices are half of the problem!" I turn to face Taylor. "I read the other day that there are 250 kinds of toothpaste, for crying out loud. And let's not even talk about Oreos, now that they've got double-frosting, mint, minis, peanut butter. . . ."

My voice fades under the roars of appreciative laughter. Taylor laughs, too, and smiles at me. And I'm kind of sorry some of this is at her expense.

When I swing back in my chair, I see that Mitch is still staring at me, not laughing.

"So what can we do about this stress? How do we live with it?"

The room grows silent, as if Mitch's somber mood is too strong for our attempts at laughter. In my head, I hear him say, *Sometimes people need a little help.*

Taylor raises her hand again. "God. Jesus."

A couple of kids groan.

"Don't swear!" Tyrone mutters. A few chuckle.

Some of the back-row guys holler, "Chicks! Parties!"

Mitch, unmoved, still fixing me with his stare, says, "Or you can stumble along, dreading one day at a time."

At the end of English, Mitch passes out scripts to everyone who wants to try out for *As You Like It*. He sets auditions for a week from Friday, giving us an extra week to worry. It's unbelievable how many people take scripts as they file out—Tressa, Brianna, Rebecca. Even Miranda takes one, reaching without looking, as if she's shoplifting.

Mitchell Wade has no idea what stress is.

■ ■ ■

By lunchtime, everybody is getting on my nerves. I've snapped at Miranda, Tressa, D.J., and our econ teacher. I don't just have an *edge* on. I'm *all* edges. I'm a walking drawerful of razor-sharp knives ripping through the day. Smart people stay away.

■   ■   ■

After school Dylan offers me a ride, and I take him up on it since I can't find Sammy anywhere. I've almost gone the whole day without anything, not even aspirin. And my head is throbbing like bongos.

"You okay, Kyra?"

Truth is, I don't feel that hot. I wish I could just smooth out the edges, just for a couple of hours. Smiling, I turn to Dylan and unbraid my braids. My hair falls past my shoulders in little waves. "There. Is that better?"

Dylan's flung his books in the backseat, and I spy a copy of the *As You Like It* script.

"Dylan! Are you trying out for the play?" I try to think all the way back to kindergarten, and I can't remember a single time that Dylan Gray stood onstage.

His face reddens when he answers, and he looks so cute I could hug him. "Well . . . I don't know. I mean, I guess I might."

"You *should!*" I say, giving him a little shoulder punch.

"I've never tried out for anything, except football. I know I won't have time for anything like this in college. Dad says I can take off work when I need to—not that I'll get the part or anything." He turns onto our street, slowing down at the deer crossing. "So I thought, now or never." He grins over at me, showing off his dimple. "Just don't make fun of me Friday. Promise?"

"No way! And I'll flatten anybody who does.

I think it's great, Dylan. Good for you!" I'm already worrying about his tryout. I don't want him to be disappointed. Dylan is just so *Dylan* that I can't picture him onstage or anywhere as someone else. "What part are you going for?"

"I didn't say I was *going* for anything. I just thought it would be fun to try out."

"Yeah, yeah. I'm just saying you might check out some of the smaller male roles—like Jaques or Duke Senior or Duke Frederick . . . or even one of the servants or shepherds. Everybody and his brother will try out for Orlando, the lead male."

"Not I!" he says dramatically, one hand smacked over his heart. "In the authentic Shakespearean tradition, *I* shall audition for nothing less than the role of the fair Rosalind!"

"Great!" I slug him with my script. "That's all I need—more competition."

We laugh together, and it feels like the first time I've laughed in weeks, maybe months, like the laughter's coming from a different place than my school and date laughs.

Dylan pulls into his driveway, and Bethany and Bag come running to greet us. Dylan's the one who came up with the name for their mutt—*Bag*, as in *Doggie Bag*. Bethany wanted to name him "Kathy." So I guess Bag got the lesser of two evils.

"Mom picked *me* up!" Bethany says, lunging into her brother's arms. He swings her in a circle and sets her down. Bag scratches at Dylan's leg, begging to be picked up, too.

"So *that's* why you beat me home, you rascal!" Dylan picks up Bag and ruffles Bethany's hair.

Bethany runs to my side of the car and gives me a hug. She lifts my greasy, wavy hair and lets it go. "What happened to your hair?"

"Thanks a lot, Bethie," I say, tickling her until she runs for cover in the garage. I turn to Dylan, who's still holding the barking Doggie Bag. "Guess I better let you go work on Rosalind's lines."

"Guess so," he answers in a falsetto that makes Bethany and me laugh.

I fish out my key and head for my house. From the front step I can see that no lights are on. I unlock the door and stand there, my hand on the cold brass doorknob. I think I'm afraid, but I'm not sure of what. Not the boogeyman. Not even a flesh-and-blood intruder. The only crime in Macon is an occasional shoplifting, if you don't count Miranda's fashion statements.

Glancing back at the Grays', I consider locking my door and running over to their house. I could say that I couldn't get the door unlocked. Or I could make up something about helping Dylan get ready for tryouts.

But I have homework. I'm already behind in econ. And besides, this is crazy. I've come home alone a thousand times.

Taking a deep breath, I open the door and step in, shutting the door behind me. "Hello? Anybody home?" The house feels colder than usual. And quieter.

Flipping on the TV, I turn up the volume and let

the CNN voices tell me about the world's tragedies while I sit at the dining table, out of viewing range, and pull out my econ book. The TV words bounce off the white walls and mix with the words in my econ book so that none of them makes sense. But they press against my skull and stir up my headache again. And I wish it would stop. *Leave me alone.*

And all I want to do is run upstairs to the orange plastic bottle. There. I said it.

But it doesn't mean I'm hooked or anything. I'm not going upstairs, not opening the orange bottle, not taking the Zanax. I'm doing my homework.

I make myself think about history. I got a B on the quiz. I should have been happy with it. I barely looked at the material. But I want an A in that class.

I have to get back to econ. Only I can't focus on the economic statistics of the postwar generation. I've read the same paragraph three times.

I scoot my chair back, the legs screaming against the tile floor, making the sound my mother hates. I push the chair in and pull it out again, making it scream louder than CNN. Instead of running upstairs—which, okay, is what I really want to do—I cross into the kitchen, snatch the wall phone, and dial Dylan's number. I didn't feel like this when I was in Dylan's car.

The phone rings once . . . twice . . . three times . . . four—

"Hello?" It's Mrs. Gray, and she sounds out of breath.

I don't know what to say. The Grays, and their home, suddenly feel a thousand miles away.

"Hello?" she says again, not angry like I would be. I hang up.

The phone cord is tangled, wrapped around my arm. So I know I must have been fooling with it. I free myself and sit back down to econ.

Stress. It's everywhere—in the *As You Like It* script, in my econ book, hiding inside my house. Even the TV voices can't take the silence out of the house.

I need to finish econ and get going on chem.

Way back in my brain somewhere I hear Taylor saying, *God. Jesus.* I hear Dylan, after we took Bethany to emergency, saying, *I think you know how we get through it.* And I'd like to pray to God, to Jesus, and ask them to take the edge off so I can get my homework done and stop aching.

But I can't. It feels fake.

Sometimes people need a little help.

I need a little help. *Now.*

I put down my pen and stretch my arms. Then I slip out of my chair, without making a sound, and stroll to the stairs—no rush here. I'm not jonesing for a stupid Zanax or anything. It's not even a *drug*, not like people mean when they talk about drugs. My own mother, who won't even say darn, takes Zanax. It's probably more psychological than anything.

But this time, after I pop open the plastic bottle, I shake out two pills. And I take them both.

16

For days, all anybody can talk about is Tryout
Friday. That's what Mitch calls it. I have never
seen kids get so involved in a school play. And
it's Shakespeare! It feels like Sammy's the only
one in the whole senior class who isn't trying out.

So on Tuesday before auditions, I decide my little
brother has sat on the sidelines long enough. The
end of lunch period, I spot him goofing off with
Tyrone and a couple of guys.

"Sammy!" I make a circle with my thumb and
index finger and blow. I have the best whistle of
anyone in our school, if I do say so myself.

Dozens of heads turn. But I can see Sammy
knows it's me. He makes a show of craning his long
neck around, surveying the cafeteria as if he didn't
know exactly where to find me.

"Come here, you idiot!" I shout.

Half a dozen guys raise their eyebrows at me. Hale Ramsey even points to himself.

"No. *That* idiot."

Finally Sammy waves wildly at me, like he hasn't seen me in years. "Sis!" he shouts, taking off at a run. He leaps over somebody's backpack, sprints, and dives to our table.

"Slow down, Mr. James!" cries Mr. Grant, monitor for the day.

Sammy looks duly repentant. "Sorry, sir!"

Mr. Grant just nods, although he'd have given anyone else detention.

"It's my long-lost sister!" Sammy grins down at me, pretending to be on the verge of tears. An actor, he's not.

"Down, Sammy," I command.

He squishes in between Miranda and me. "Might I assume you have food of which you wish to dispose?" he asks with mock dignity.

"Are you kidding?" Miranda holds up her nibbled-at sandwich. "Shelby made my lunch today. Now I remember why I stopped asking her to. I wouldn't even offer this sandwich to Brianna."

Sammy sniffs the unidentified sandwich filling and wrinkles his nose. "That is so wrong. In so many ways." He turns to my tray.

"Don't look at Kyra for leftovers," Miranda warned. "She's outeating D.J., no contest."

My tray is empty of all traces of food. I did eat everything, including Miranda's dry brownie. And my voracious appetite has nothing to do with impressing D.J., even though I did eat his apple-sauce. Since Monday I've been famished, overcome with waves of gnawing hunger. So now I have one more thing to stress about. But I plan to quit taking the pills as soon as tryouts are over. And I think my appetite will return to human size.

I've been letting myself have two pills a day. That's it. That's all. I tried taking one in the morning and one at night, but it didn't work. So I take them together. And I'm fine. Most of the day, I'm pretty fine.

"You had two bowls of cereal this morning, *big* sister! So I guess I know where the chocolate ice cream went."

He tries to pat my stomach, but I'm too fast for him. "Cut it out, Sammy! I got you over here so I could help you out."

Sammy gets his lost-puppy look. "I wasn't aware I needed help."

"Miranda," I ask, ignoring my brother, "what would you say about a guy who's too uptight to try out for a high school play?"

"I'd say that guy is without excuse. Nobody—and I mean *no body*—could have more stage fright than I do. And I'm trying out . . . I think."

I kick her under the table. We've already agreed that Miranda will try out for the role of Celia. I'll handle Rosalind.

"I mean, of course I'm trying out!" Miranda exclaims. "You should do it, Sammy. It'll be fun."

"Not my thing." Sammy starts to get up, but we each grab an arm and won't let him.

"Look, little brother. I'll help. I'll give you the benefit of my years of experience, not to mention my future profession."

"Kind offer, Sis. No doubt about it. Still, I've got ball and biking and—"

I yawn, a big long yawn.

"Sorry I'm so boring," Sammy says.

"Not you." I yawn again, so my words get ground together. "I'm just tired." That's true enough. I'm tired almost all the time. And I'm not sleeping well at night. Once Tryout Friday is over, I'll get my life back to normal.

I try again. "Come on, Sammy. Loosen up. It's our senior year! People are starting to talk. I can't have my twin on the verge of geekdom. Time to try some new things, stretch those little wings."

Sammy moves his lips to one side, and I know I've almost got him. If Sammy were a class, I'd have an A in him.

"I meant what I said about helping you for the tryouts. I'll coach lines with you."

He narrows his eyes to slits. "You'd read lines with me?"

I nod.

"Nah. I don't think so. You'd just get all mad and mean if I didn't perform to your standards." He turns on the charm and takes Miranda's hand. "Now, if the lovely Ms. Miranda were available for intensive coaching, I would find it hard to refuse."

"Sold!" I exclaim. "The lovely Miranda would be honored, right?"

"Honored maybe," Miranda says. "Helpful, no. I can't even read my own lines without tripping on my tongue."

"We shall muddle through it together," Sammy says, getting to his feet without releasing Miranda's hand. He bends down and kisses the back of her hand. "After zee school. Today, *oui?*" It's as good a French accent as Sammy can give.

"Maybe we should rethink this," I mutter.

"What?" Sammy says. I've muttered near his bad ear.

I take advantage of the second chance and say, "Great attitude, little brother!"

Sammy heads out. *"Au Riviera!"*

"Think *English*, Sammy!" Miranda calls after him. "Not French! Shakespeare!"

When Sammy's gone, I catch Miranda glancing around. I'm thinking she's checking out the cafeteria for Ryan, but I don't ask. Miranda and I work best when we stay on the surface of things. I'm not crazy about Ryan Emerson. I'm not sure if Miranda knows I dated him our sophomore year. He's got a temper. Miranda's been acting kind of funny lately, and I hope they're not serious. I also hope Ryan realizes she and Sammy are just old friends.

■   ■   ■

I barely see Sammy until Tryout Friday. Tuesday night I get my car back from the shop, so I don't even ride in with him to school. Between his basketball practices, biking with Mitch, and practicing his lines with Miranda, my brother isn't around the house much.

Friday afternoon, a couple dozen kids line up outside the gym before sixth hour. They're all trying out for the play. Sammy and Miranda are there, but they keep letting people in front of them so they can be at the end of the line. They look pretty serious as they whisper lines back and forth.

Principal Wilcox granted us permission to hold the tryouts during school time because there's a game in the gym tonight. Mitch told us he'd been "severely chastised" for not consulting the official school schedule before arranging tryouts.

Our gym is nothing to brag about—basketball court, silver bench bleachers, that sweaty gym smell that only goes away with ammonia, which is just as bad. But the stage is pretty cool. And the curtains rock—thick red velvet.

I was doing okay until I came to the gym. Now, seeing how nervous everybody is, some of their anxiety rubs off on me. I already wish I hadn't goaded Sammy into trying out. If he blows it, he'll just laugh it off and turn it into a great story. But if I blow it, I'd just as soon my little brother wouldn't witness my downfall.

Mitch comes to the doorway and ushers us in. We stick together, like frightened children. Folding chairs are still set up from the cheesy assembly we had in the morning. We fall in to the first two or three rows.

Tyrone, Hillbilly Hale, and a couple of other guys are already sprawled in the back row, no doubt waiting for us to mess up so they can make fun of the losers. I think this is their gym hour, and I wonder where the rest of the class is and why these guys aren't with them. Tyrone's hard to figure out. He acts like he and Hale are blood brothers, but he and Mitch seem to be buddy-buddy, too. I really don't care what Tyrone Larson thinks about me, but on the other hand, I still wish he weren't here.

Dylan comes jogging down the aisle, script in hand. I wave and scoot over so he can sit next to me. He slides in just as Mitch is beginning his director's spiel.

"Did I miss anything?" Dylan whispers. "Couldn't get my locker open."

I laugh. For as long as we've had lockers, Dylan has had trouble opening his.

"Who gets to go first?" Tressa shouts after Mitch finishes welcoming us. She's front-row center, wearing pin-striped capri pants with ankle-strap, patent pumps I've never seen before and would like to see on my own feet.

"Random order, Tressa," Mitch answers, pulling a little address book out of his pocket.

Tressa hops out of her seat and tries to peek at the tiny black book, but Mitch holds it so she can't. "Top secret," he warns.

Miranda and Sammy slip in behind Dylan and me. Sammy leans forward. "I can't believe you talked me into this, Kyra!"

"He's more nervous than I am," Miranda says, leaning back in her chair. "And that's saying something."

"Help me out here, Dylan, my man!" Sammy pleads. "You are the king of cool." He rubs elbows with Dylan. "Rub off on me!"

Dylan blushes. "I'm shaking in my boots, Sam. But we'll both be okay."

"Can we pray for this thing?" Sammy's wound tight, and he asks it half-joking. Or maybe not. I can't tell.

Sammy and I haven't talked about God or prayer for a long time. We haven't prayed together since we had bunk beds and had to say our prayers every night with our parents standing over us.

"We can definitely pray for this thing," Dylan says. But he's so natural saying it that nobody seems to feel weird. Or maybe we're all too nervous.

"Give me five minutes to finish setting up!" Mitch hollers over the murmuring, private conversations buzzing through the gym.

"Let's go over our lines one more time," Sammy suggests, scooting his chair around to face Miranda. "And remember to talk to my right ear, will you?"

"Come on, Dylan." I stand up, taking his arm. "Let's check out the stage, get the feel of it."

In the pocket of my suede jacket are two Zanax. I snatched them last night and have kept them hidden inside my zipper pocket all day. I've successfully fought off every temptation to take either pill early. They have to be working when I try out. I just wish I knew when my turn was so I could time it perfectly.

Dylan and I climb the little steps on the far side of the stage and come out behind the curtain.

"Smell it, Dylan!" I love the whiff of the old wood floor, the musty-curtain smell.

"Pepperoni pizza?" Dylan ventures.

"No!" Although I do smell leftover lunch. "The smell of the stage. If I had a bottle, I'd save this theater smell for Bethany." Maybe I really do love acting. Maybe it's something I'm meant to do, to be. Maybe it's not just something I've drifted into by default, or the thing my parents wanted for their daughter.

But I don't know. I don't know how to know.

Dylan's pacing. "I'm with Sammy. Why on earth did I sign up for this?"

"You'll be fine, Dylan. You can use your script, you know."

"Oh, I'll use my script all right—to hide my face."

I dodge the curtain rope to get to him. "Take it easy, Dylan. It's only a high-school tryout."

"Easy for you to say."

"Not really."

Dylan stops pacing and stares at me until I look away. "What do you mean, Kyra?"

"Nothing." I chuckle, but it sounds fake, even to me. I touch my pocket and feel the two tiny lumps inside.

"What's up?" Dylan still hasn't looked away.

"Dylan, you're being weird. Nothing's up."

He doesn't smile, doesn't let me brush it off. "Something's going on with you. I just wish you'd talk to me about it."

But I can't. If I start letting the things inside me come out, I might not be able to stop them. Or I might find out there's nothing inside me . . . that there *is* no real Kyra James.

"The only thing wrong with me is that I'm thirsty and it's Tryout Friday!" I shove him toward the steps. "Okay. So I'm a little nervous. You got me. So are you." I keep us moving. "Now scoot! Save my seat. I'm going to get a drink. I'll be right down."

I watch Dylan as he retraces his steps and takes his seat. Then he does his sneaky thing again, like he did in the hospital waiting room. He leans forward, elbows on his knees, hands clasped around the back of his neck. Anybody else looking at him would think he's resting or going over his lines. But I know he's praying.

Pray for me, too, Dylan.

I hurry to the water fountain at the back of the stage, pull out the pills, and swallow.

By the time Mitch finally comes back and calls us to order, Dylan is 10 times calmer than I am. As he chats with kids around us, I sneak peeks at him—his smile, his dimple.

There's no reason I can't pray, too. It's not like I never pray. At night sometimes I'll pray for my family, that they'll be safe. Or when somebody's sick, like Grandma James was last year. Or Bethany. I just haven't been praying enough to feel I've got a right to ask for things like a part in the play, the lead in the play.

Help me calm down, God.

But that's all I can say. And I feel weird for praying at all, like I was just copying Dylan or maybe covering all the bases, hedging my bets.

"Tressa, you're up first," Mitch announces.
He's wearing khakis with a navy sweater, sleeves pushed up his tan arms.

Tressa jumps up from her chair. "Me? I can't believe I'm first!"

"Go, Tressa!" Dylan shouts.

I can't help but wonder if Tressa really would have been first if she hadn't pestered Mitch to death.

She trots to the stage, faces us, and then hoists herself up to sit on the edge of the stage. Looking ready to give a Macon Tiger cheer, she bounds to her feet. "Oops! I forgot my script."

Brianna tosses it up to her.

Mitch stands below the stage and reads Duke Frederick's lines, cuing Tressa for Celia's dialogues. I can tell Tressa has practiced a lot. She delivers most of her lines without looking at the script. But even though she's memorized nearly every line, she sounds as if she's reading.

"Very good," Mitch says, without much enthusiasm. "Thanks, Tressa. It's tough to lead off."

Tressa is undaunted as she reverses her motions to get down from the stage, sitting on the edge, and then jumping. She lands in front of Dylan and me.

"Good job, Tressa," Dylan says, like he means it. "You didn't even look scared."

"Really?" She fiddles with a lock of her red hair. "Did you think I was any good?" She glances at me and waits.

"Awesome!" I say. "And you really looked great up there, too. Those shoes are sweet!"

She struts back to her chair. "Mitch, when will we find out who gets what role?"

"Well," Mitch says, "I thought I'd at least wait until the others have read, if that's all right with you, Tressa."

We laugh, but it's nervous laughter, broken and full of air.

Rebecca won't let it go. "Come on, Mitch! When are you going to tell us who wins?"

"*Wins*?" Mitch repeats. "You mean who gets the parts of Celia and Rosalind and Orlando—"

"Yeah, yeah. When can we find out?" Rebecca demands.

"I'll know my main actors and actresses by the time we finish Tryout Friday." Mitch smiles at us. We're his audience. "No reason why I should keep

you in suspense. I'll let you know on the main
parts when we're done here. Deal?"

Mrs. Overstreet always typed a cast list and
posted it on the bulletin board the day after tryouts.
At least that way kids didn't have an audience when
they found out they hadn't *won*.

"And don't forget," Mitch continues, like an
afterthought, while we're soaking up the fact that
it will really be all over this afternoon, "there are
plenty of smaller parts. No small parts, only small
players, right? Plus, we'll need a light crew and
scenery people."

If Mitch puts me on light crew, I'll drop out of
high school.

I can hear Tressa babbling on to Manny, who is
sitting next to her. "Do you think he's saying something about me? Like maybe I have a big role? Or
what if he means I have to have a small role? Do
you think he's really saying that?"

I'm glad we're four chairs down from Tressa.
She's making me jittery, in spite of the Zanax. I try
to tune her out.

Brianna goes next. Her performance as Rosalind
is a repeat of her class reading. She can't stop laughing, and only about a third of the words come out
so we can understand them.

Dylan laughs along with her, and he seems to
be the only person in the audience Bri looks at. My
guess is that she can see, or hear, that Dylan is the
only one who's laughing *with* her. The rest of us are
laughing *at* her.

I can't help it. The way she tries to muffle

laughter and it spits through anyway. Still, I'd almost feel sorry for her if she didn't appear to be enjoying herself so much.

Two more girls go, and I've concluded that Mitch must be auditioning all the female roles first. It's a good break for me because already I feel the Zanax wearing off.

"Kyra James?" Mitch calls, as if he's not sure whether I'm here or not.

Behind me, Sammy and Miranda whisper something, but I don't get it.

I feel Dylan's hand on my arm. "You'll do great, Kyra."

My brain spins Rosalind's lines in my head. In class Mitch gave us three scenes to work on for the audition. So far he's had all the Rosalinds read the same passage. I've been saying those lines over with each tryout, so I'm sure I won't need my script.

But when I climb the stage, Mitch says, "Let me hear you do Rosalind's last speech, when she's alone onstage for the epilogue." He sits down.

For a second I think I'll have Dylan toss me my script just like Tressa had Brianna toss hers. I glance at Dylan. He's already got hold of my script, ready to hand it over.

Then the lines start to come to me. I open my mouth and say them:

> *It is not the fashion to see the lady the*
> *epilogue; but it is no more*
> *unhandsome than to see the lord the*
> *prologue. . . .*

The words keep coming, and I forget everything else.

> . . . *I charge you, O women, for the love*
> *you bear to men, to like as much of*
> *this play as please you. And I charge*
> *you, O men, for the love you bear to*
> *women—as I perceive by your*
> *simpering none of you hates them—*
> *that between you and the women the*
> *play may please. . . .*

As I speak for Rosalind, it's more like I'm listening to her, melting into her. And when I'm finished,
it feels like waking up. It takes me a second before
I have all my senses.

Everybody, except Tyrone and Hale, applauds.
Sammy and Miranda give me standing ovations,
and Dylan's right there with them, cheering for me.

Then I spot Mitch, still sitting with his arms
crossed. Only when I look right at him does he smile,
politely.

"Thank you, Kyra." He stands up and turns
around to face the bleachers. "I think we ought to
hold the applause though, or we'll be here all night.
And Principal Wilcox will fire me."

I scurry off the stage and take my seat next to
Dylan.

Maybe I wasn't as good as I thought I was.

I feel pats on my back from Miranda and Sammy.

"That was so tight!" Dylan whispers.

But they've never been in a play. They don't
know as much as Mitch does about what's good and

what's not. My stomach's churning, and I feel like I'm going to be sick. I wish I could do it over. Try again. Do it better.

■ ■ ■

When Mitch finally calls Miranda's name, she and Sammy both stand up. Dylan and I crane around to watch them as, together, they slip through the row and up to Mitch.

"I have to try out with my partner," Miranda says.

"We're almost ready for the guys," Mitch says. "Sam can go right after you."

"We'll save you time," Sammy says. "Two tryouts for the price of one?"

"Go, Sammy!" Jamal shouts.

"Did they tell you they were doing this?" Dylan whispers.

I shake my head. And I realize how little either one of them tells me anything.

"We're a team," Miranda says.

Mitch grins, then sits down.

Sammy lifts Miranda by her waist and sets her onstage. She takes a step, slips, and almost crashes. I hear Hale's laugh from the peanut gallery, and I glare at him.

Sammy vaults to the stage in a single bound.

"Try Act Four, Scene Three," Mitch calls up to them.

Miranda and Sammy grin at each other, as if they're glad he chose that one. They're giggling, and it reminds me of when we were eight or 10 and best friends. We told each other everything then, or it seemed like that.

I flip through the script until I see it. They're reading for Oliver and Celia. That's good. Sammy could be the only one trying out for Oliver's role.

Miranda's wearing black stretch pants that her mom probably picked out for her. But she's got on the cool white blouse I helped her pick out from Kaufman's. It looks good. Sammy's honored the occasion with blue jeans and a white T-shirt.

I want them to do really well. Out of the corner of my eye, I see Dylan's hand resting on his knee. And for some reason, I want to take his hand and hold it until auditions are over.

Kyra James, get a grip. Dylan is your buddy.

Sammy clears his throat. Miranda stares at her long feet.

"Anytime," Mitch says.

Miranda nods, and Sammy begins:

> Oliver: Good morrow, fair ones. Pray you,
> if you know, where in the purlius of
> this forest stands a sheepcote fenced
> about with olive trees?

Miranda snaps Celia's answer back to Sammy. They bounce the lines back and forth like that, not missing a beat. They don't try for a British accent, and they sound like high-school kids giving Shake-speare a chance. But there's something about the chemistry, the way they play off each other, that works.

"They're good, right?" Dylan whispers, shifting in his seat.

I nod without taking my eyes off them.

When they finish the scene, I jump out of my chair and applaud. "Yeah! Way to go!"

Dylan gets up and we both cheer, ignoring Mitch's no-applause request. Some of the other kids holler too.

Miranda and Sammy run offstage, down the steps, and back to their seats.

Dylan and I high-five them. I don't think I've ever seen Sammy's face this red. Mrs. Overstreet would call it a cliché. But she'd be proud of Sammy. And Miranda.

Two more girls come up and say they want to try out, even though they haven't signed up. Mitch lets them, but they speak so softly you can barely hear them.

"Now for the gents!" Mitch announces.

One after the other, the boys take turns reading onstage. Only a couple of them have bothered to memorize their lines. Brent has the best audition, in my opinion. And Jamal isn't half-bad either. Most of them read for the part of Orlando, with only Benjamin Bean reading for the same role as Sammy, the Oliver part.

Mitch calls guy after guy, not even pretending to go by a list. A couple of times he glances at Dylan, and I'm sure he's going to call him. But he doesn't. It's like he's leaving Dylan sitting there, in the front row, on purpose.

I've wondered before how Dylan got along with

Mitch. At least half the things Mitch says in our class, I know Dylan would have disagreed with. And he's no wimp when it comes to defending his beliefs and opinions.

"How do you and Mitch get along in class?" I whisper to Dylan, as Manny finishes stumbling over Orlando's lines.

"We don't always see eye to eye," Dylan admits. "That's for sure. Sometimes—"

"Dylan Gray?" Mitch calls.

Everyone else has auditioned. But nobody's left the gym, not even Tyrone and Hale.

Dylan stands up.

"Why don't you read from the first scene, page four?" Mitch moves close to the stage. "I'll be Oliver, and you can be Orlando."

Everyone else has read from Orlando's later scene with Rosalind, and I wonder why Mitch is making Dylan do *this* scene.

I want to stop Dylan from taking the stage. What if he makes a fool of himself? Tyrone and Hale would love to lead the heckling. I knew Dylan decided to read for Orlando. I should have tried harder to get him to go for one of the other roles, but I was too busy worrying about my own audition. If he blows this and ends up with nothing, it's going to be my fault.

Dylan, script in hand, climbs to the stage and takes his spot front and center. From the stage he looks down on Mitch. "Anytime, Mr. Wade," he says politely.

I think I see anger flash in Mitch's eyes before he smiles. Nobody else calls him anything but Mitch.

Mitch, as Oliver, reads the first line, throwing himself into it more than he did with any of us.

> Oliver: *Now, sir, what make you here?*
> Orlando: *Nothing. I am not taught to make anything.*
> Oliver: *What mar you then, sir?*
> Orlando: *Marry, sir, I am helping you to mar that which God made, a poor unworthy brother of yours, with idleness.*

> Oliver: Marry, sir, be better employed,
> and be nought awhile.
> Orlando: Shall I keep your hogs, and eat
> husks with them? What prodigal
> portion have I spent, that I should
> come to such penury?
> Oliver: Know you where you are, sir?
> Orlando: O sir, very well; here in your
> orchard.
> Oliver: Know you before whom, sir?
> Orlando: Ay, better than him I am before
> knows me.

Mitch spits out the words, as if he really is angry with Dylan. But Dylan matches him, firing the lines back. And he does it in a British accent! *My* Dylan! I'm amazed. This isn't the sweet, kind Dylan I've known my whole life. He sounds filled with rage, and so does Mitch. And they both might have been born in Stratford-upon-Avon.

When the scene ends, total silence fills the auditorium. Even Tyrone and Hale don't make a sound.

I'm awed, astounded. And from the looks on the faces around me, so is everyone. Who would have suspected our Dylan had it in him?

I'm the first to break the spell. "Unbelievable, Dylan! Way to go!" I clap.

Then the gym fills with applause. Some are standing, some sitting. Sammy and I cheer as Dylan hurries offstage and slinks back to his seat.

"Was it really okay?" he asks. He's not fishing

for a compliment. I can spot that a mile off. He really doesn't know.

I sit next to him. "Dylan, it was fantastic! Where did you learn to do a British accent?"

He grins. "Studied at Masterpiece Theatre. Got my PBS."

"Everybody quiet down, please," Mitch says, not saying a word to Dylan. "I think we're going to have a powerful play by spring. I admit I had my doubts about what good could come out of Macon, Iowa."

We chuckle in the right place for him.

"Every one of you who tried out today has reason to be proud. *You* are the ones who will make it in life. You're not afraid to take a chance, to risk, to live."

We're listening totally, just like we do in class.

"We'll work together on this play and show this little provincial town what we can do." He's quiet for a minute. "I know you're anxious to know what I've decided about the roles, so I'll get on with it. I'm just announcing major parts. So don't forget what I said about having a place for everybody."

"Brent, I want you to play the role of Duke Senior. I'm confident you'll bring power to that part. Congratulations."

We clap weakly, but Brent's face contorts with his disappointment. He'd tried out for Orlando's part.

Jamie Cantrell, Miranda's ex-boyfriend, a nice guy Sammy used to hang out with, gets the part of Duke Frederick. He reacts totally the opposite of Brent. Jamie shoots his fist in the air and shouts, "Yes! I can't believe I got a part!"

Mitch turns in our direction, and I hold my breath. "I'm going to have to go with Sam James in the role of Oliver. . . . "

I gasp. Sammy did it!

"And Miranda as Celia."

Dylan and I turn to give them high-fives.

"You guys!" I feel electric, with chills racing through my bones. "That is so great! I'm so proud of you two!"

Miranda looks stunned. Her mouth sags, and she hasn't blinked. Sammy's laughing, like he just got away with another tardy pass.

Mitch grabs our attention again. "That leaves Rosalind and Orlando."

I can't stop myself. My hand reaches over and takes Dylan's hand.

"The part of Rosalind goes to . . ." Mitch turns toward the other end of the auditorium, as if looking for someone. We're still, waiting. His head slowly turns until he's facing straight out, at Tressa, at Brianna. Then he turns our way. " . . . our own Kyra James!"

Mitch liked me! He liked my performance.

Dylan squeezes my hand. Miranda and Sammy pound me so hard on the back, they almost knock me out of the chair.

I have a second of intense satisfaction. I tried out for the lead, and I got it. With a new teacher. With more girls trying for the part than ever. I won.

But in the next instant, something close to panic starts in my throat and seeps into my body, like a purple dye, reaching into all directions at once.

What if I blow it? What if all of these people depend on me to be wonderful as Rosalind, and I let them down? My parents. Sammy and Miranda. Mitch.

"Hey, you won," Dylan says, releasing my hand. "You look like you lost."

I try to shake it off, to feel good about this again. "I'm . . . I'm just relieved."

"Could have fooled me," Dylan says.

"We're not done yet, people!" Mitch shouts.

Tyrone and Hale are already moving toward the exit. They keep going. But the rest of us quiet down.

"There were some great performances here for Orlando's part. And some of you earned other roles. So hang on until Monday, okay?"

Without looking at Dylan, I reach for his hand again. My fingers close over his. *Come on, Dylan!*

"I think we'll all have to admit that there's only one true Orlando here," Mitch says.

It has to go to Dylan.

"Dylan Gray," Mitch says with no emotion.

"Yes!" I'm out of my seat. Then I'm standing on my chair. "Dylan! Dylan! Dylan!"

He pulls me back down, and I grab him in a bear hug. Other arms wrap around us, Miranda and Sammy joining in a four-way hug that could choke a bear.

And I think I've never been this happy, at least, not in a long, long time.

Thank you, God. It's like I'm bursting, so thankful it comes out in a prayer. And that feels good, really good. Because I can't remember the last time I really thanked God for anything.

The gym has pretty much cleared by the time we loosen our hug.

"Hey!" I cry, not wanting to let any of them go. They're all a head taller than I am, so I feel like I'm in the middle of a huddle. "Let's celebrate! After the game tonight! Let's go out together."

Sammy lets go of my shoulder and runs his hand over his hair. "Sorry. Can't. Not tonight."

"Me either." Miranda breaks away and grabs her script and bookbag. "Got a date with Ryan after the game."

I turn to Dylan. I don't have a date after the game. D.J. is going to some drag-racing thing his brother's into. He won't even be at the game. "Looks like just you and me, big fella."

"Sorry, Kyra," Dylan says, not looking at me. "I've already got plans for tonight."

I feel as if the cold, refreshing waters that have been rushing through me have been shut off with one hard twist of a faucet. And just like that, all of the joy and happiness end. Gone.

"No big deal," I say, punching Dylan's arm, smiling. "And good for you, Dylan! Have fun. I'll see you at the game probably. I'll be the one jumping around at halftime and screaming cheers."

He grins, dimple shining.

I say congratulations to Miranda and Sammy again and stroll out of the auditorium alone.

It may be my best performance of the day.

Grrr! Tigers! *Beat Wildcats!*
Go, Tigers! You're the best!
Fight, fight, fight for Macon High!
Victory is our battle cry!

Nobody else on the squad can do a back flip, so I do three of them in a row and let the crowd cheer their approval. Sometimes I like cheering, and sometimes I think I'd rather be home watching *Buffy the Vampire Slayer* reruns and eating microwave popcorn in my pj's.

But I make sure nobody would guess this to look at me.

"You *have* to teach me how to do that!" Megan says as the buzzer sounds and we jog off the court.

Megan swung by my house earlier and picked me

up for the big game. She and I are the only cheer-leaders without dates tonight. Maybe we should start our own club, *Cheerleaders without Partners,* like *Parents without Partners.*

"Sure," I say, although I'm not sure I can help her pull off a back flip. She's put on about 15 pounds since last year, and she can barely manage the cart-wheels. But I don't say this.

Brianna chimes in. She's always teasing Megan about her weight. "You know what they say, Megan. Inside every fat girl there's a skinny girl crying to get out."

"Yeah," I shoot back, knowing Megan won't have a comeback quick enough. "So do like Brianna does. Feed that skinny girl chocolate and she'll shut up. Right, Bri?"

Brianna forces a fake smile. We all know she scarfs Snickers every chance she gets.

"Thanks, Kyra," Megan whispers.

We take our spots on the sideline, and I gaze at the crowd, scanning faces for Dylan. I don't see him though. Maybe the *plans* he already had for tonight don't include the basketball game. Maybe he'd promised to do something with Bethany.

"Look who's coming in over there," Tressa says, elbowing me, then pointing to the doors.

Dylan walks in with Taylor by his side. She's wearing jeans and a red sweater with tennis shoes. She looks cute.

"Did you know they were going out, Kyra?" Tressa asks.

"What, Dylan and Taylor?" I act uninterested.

"Dylan said something about tonight. They're not exactly *going out.*"

"Looks that way to me," Brianna offers.

I shrug. Out of the corner of my eye, I see them climb the bleachers, Dylan's hand holding Taylor's elbow as they make their way nearly to the top.

The bleachers are filled with couples of all ages, as if they're just waiting to march two-by-two into the ark and I'm the only one left outside without a partner. It feels like everyone at the game—even the other side—knows Kyra James couldn't get a date to a home game.

"Where's D.J.?" Tressa asks.

I suspect she already knows, but I answer anyway. "With Eric, his brother, at a boring drag race."

"I *love* drag races!" Megan exclaims. "Too bad you didn't get to go along."

Somebody scores, and we race onto the court to lead the screaming.

By the time the first quarter ends, we're down by eight. I cheer and yell as if it matters. Sammy's having a good game, and so is Jamal. But the rest of the team can't hit the basket, and the other team's sinking everything.

I do another back flip and wonder if Taylor and Dylan are watching. A couple of times, I risk peeking at them. They're leaning into each other, deep in conversation. Taylor's into sports. She can probably hold her own in any basketball discussions with Dylan. I should be glad for my friend. Taylor really is Dylan's type. They might be engrossed in a conversation about God, instead of basketball, for all I know.

I feel edgy. It helps to be able to scream and throw myself around on the floor and have everyone accept it as normal cheering.

At halftime I get a bottle of water and hear my name called. I look up and see Tyrone. He thunders down the bleachers, bumping people out of the way, and drops in front of me. "So, need a ride home? Want to go to the Tiger Den after the game?"

I'm right. *Cheerleaders without Partners* must be written on my back. "I'm okay," I answer. "Megan's giving me a lift home."

Tyrone, a man of few words, eyes me carefully and then starts his bleacher climb.

Tressa and Brianna are still ignoring me. I think they're hacked off about tryouts.

I take a seat next to Megan, who must have popped a whole pack of gum into her mouth. She chews with her mouth open. As Sammy would say, "Wrong. In so many ways."

"How're y'all?" Hale Ramsey is standing in front of Megan. Hillbilly Hale, although no one with a wish for long life calls him that to his face. He's small, but he fights dirty. Probably learned it while he was in that juvenile detention center. Or maybe that's what got him sent there. Hale's wearing striped-jean bell-bottoms and a black shirt. You can tell a lot about a guy by what he puts in his hair or on his head. I've never seen Hale wear a baseball cap. If he did, it would get stuck on all that gel. Wrong. In so many ways.

"Hi, Hale," Megan replies. The wad of gum tucked

in her cheek makes her look like she's got one-sided mumps.

I nod at Hale, but I feel like sliding farther away from him.

"Y'all were jumpin' to beat the band out there. Cool as spit!"

I study my purple tennis shoes so I won't laugh. Only the suicidal laugh at the way Hale talks.

"Thanks, Hale," Megan says sweetly.

"I reckon you already got a stableful of jocks lining up to take you out after the game." He's talking to Megan, not to me.

Megan laughs softly, not saying she does have a stableful, not saying she doesn't.

"'Cause I was thinkin'," Hale drawls, "maybe we could get us something to eat over at the Den. I mean, after the game. I was fixin' to ask y'all before, but I reckon I done lost my wherefore."

Megan looks like she's not exactly sure what he said. "You want *me* to go with you to the Tiger Den?"

Hale nods. "Only . . . well, my rod's on blocks. Busted rod. We'll have to flag us a ride with somebody."

"*I* have a car!" Megan says, her eyes wide and hopeful. Then she turns to me, and her face collapses.

"No sweat," I say, feeling like I just lost my vice president of *Cheerleaders without Partners*. "I can hitch a ride home with Sammy or something. Go!"

"Okay, Hale," Megan tells him. "Thanks."

I watch Hale walk away bowlegged. The back of his black T-shirt says "Doesn't play well with others."

I don't trust Hale Ramsey. This sudden invitation seems like it's come from the foul line, if you ask me. Hale's nervous act isn't convincing. He *makes* people nervous, not the other way around.

But Megan runs off to the john to check her lipstick, and she's smiling, obviously thrilled not to be left out of after-game time. So I keep my thoughts about Hale to myself and start worrying about how I'll get home. I already know Sammy's going out with Jamal and some of the guys after the game.

"Hey, Kyra!" Dylan calls, as he and Taylor stroll our way.

Taylor smiles and lifts her hand in a single wave. "Congratulations on tryouts, Kyra."

"Thanks. *You* should have tried out, Taylor."

"Taylor works after school," Dylan answers for her. It feels like he's coming to her defense and accusing me for not working after school.

"I wouldn't have tried out no matter what," Taylor says, her smile genuine. "I'd make a fool of myself. I don't know how you do it, Kyra."

I want to not like her, but she doesn't make it easy. She's totally sincere. "I'll bet you'd surprise yourself. Like ol' Dylan." I punch his arm. Nothing but buds here.

"Believe me," Taylor says, "nobody wants to see me onstage. You're a natural, Kyra. It's a gift. Like the way you do that flip! I took gymnastics for three years when I was a kid. They gave up on me. I couldn't even do a cartwheel."

"You don't need to do cartwheels when you're a

soccer star," I counter. We're so nice, we're making me sick.

"We better get something to drink," Dylan says, taking Taylor's arm and heading out toward the vending machines. He smiles at me though, as if he's actually glad to see me, to chat with me. "See you later, Kyra. Break an ankle!" It's an old joke, a private joke. Dylan's version of the theatrical *break a leg.*

Taylor calls over her shoulder, "See you at the Den later?"

I wave. "Yeah! I'll be there!" What else am I going to say? No, I'll be holding a recruitment meeting for *Cheerleaders without Partners?*

Halftime's almost over though. I don't have a ride home, much less a ride to the Den. And I'm not walking into the Tiger Den alone.

Maybe, just this once, I could let Tyrone take me. As long as he knows it's not a date, what could it hurt?

I turn to see if I can spot Tyrone in the bleachers, and I almost run into him. He's standing behind me, close enough for me to smell his weird cologne.

"Hey." Tyrone in his talkative mode.

"What are you doing back here?"

He shrugs. "Change your mind?"

I think about saying no and sending him back to the bleachers. But I need a ride. And a partner.

"If you're going to the Den," I say reluctantly, "I could use a ride after all."

"Okay." Tyrone is not the Tiger Den kind of guy. He's never worn a Tiger T-shirt or screamed at pep rallies and games. I know he wouldn't even go to the Den if I didn't go with him.

It rankles that he's not surprised by my sudden change of heart. It's like he knows I need a ride, even though I told him I came with Megan.

"Later." He turns and heads back to the bleachers.

Suspicion spreads over me like measles. I have a bad feeling about this. Truth is, I don't want to go to the Tiger Den. And I for sure don't want to go there with Tyrone Larson. But I can't just not show up.

I lead the charge back onto the court for one last cheer before the second half starts. We end in a human pyramid, Megan on the bottom, me on top. I stand up straight on Tressa's and Brianna's backs and feel as if I'm 100 feet in the air.

And I wonder what it would feel like to dive headfirst to the floor, on purpose.

When the game ends in defeat, Tyrone is right there to collect me. I could kick myself for this one, and I can't even remember how I got myself into another "date" with Tyrone.

Mom used to tell Sammy and me, "Life is a series of choices and decisions. You have to keep on your toes for all of them."

Sammy and I used to laugh as soon as Mom turned her back. But I'd have to agree with her tonight. I have been spending way too much time flat-footed.

Since I thought I'd be going straight home after the game, I haven't brought anything to change into. So I'm stuck in the purple leotard and short wraparound skirt. Tressa and Brianna wouldn't change out of their cheerleading uniforms if a hurricane hit the cornfields of Iowa. But something about Tyrone has always made me want to cover up as much of myself as possible.

Maybe I'm too hard on the guy. I don't really know him. Part of me is even jealous of how he honestly doesn't seem to care what people think. He's no slave to fashion. He wouldn't be caught dead with a Polo pony on his shirt. The guy won't even wear T-shirts with Nike emblems.

He hasn't said a word as I gather my stuff.

"Let me get my coat and—," I start.

Tyrone hands me my coat, which he's already fetched.

We join the crowd shoving toward the doors. Outside, even with the parking lights around the school lot, stars punch through the black sky. Cold air stings my cheeks as I dash for Tyrone's car, holding my jacket closed and wishing I had gloves and jeans.

Tyrone unlocks the car while I stamp my feet and blow on my fingers to keep the circulation going. I slide in and fasten my seat belt. The car's old, which I don't care about unless the heater doesn't work. At least he has a car now. Our last "date," we walked.

Tyrone gets in and sticks the key in the ignition but doesn't turn it.

"I'm begging you to put the heater on," I say.

"I was thinking . . ." He starts the car and revs the engine. Outside, muffled voices and shouts echo across the lot. Doors slam, engines roar. "We could blow off the Tiger Den and go somewhere private."

"I don't think so." What I mean is, *Over your dead body, Tyrone.*

"I've got a six-pack wrapped in the trunk."

I shake my head, but the rest of me is already shaking. I can't even stand the taste of beer. At parties I usually pretend I like beer, then nurse one all night.

"You haven't gone teetotaler on me, have you?"

"Get real, Tyrone." I don't need Tyrone's bad press circulating.

He shrugs.

"Listen, just take me to the Den or take me home. I'm really tired." I am, too. Sleepy and tired, with my bones and muscles doing battle inside me.

Tyrone peels out of the parking lot. Gravel spits. The back wheels slide. Somebody honks. A group of kids scurry out of the way, and a red Toyota, backing out of a parking space, slams on the brakes as we speed by and bounce out to the road.

I don't say anything because I know it's Tyrone's way of telling me he's not happy with me.

"So is D.J. going to be mad at me when word gets back that you and I went out?"

"In the first place, you and I are *not* going out. And in the second place, D.J. doesn't own me."

"I thought you and D.J. were partying tomorrow night."

I hate the way Tyrone knows everything about everything. And acts like he knows me. "So what?"

"Easy, girl." He puts both hands up in defense position. I wish he'd put them back on the steering wheel.

Neither of us speaks until he pulls up to the curb
two blocks from the Tiger Den. I don't know why
he doesn't park behind the Den and save us the sub-
zero hiking experience.

Kids are already flowing into the Den when we
get there. Through the window, I can see that the
booths are already filled. A couple of juniors wave,
and I wave back.

The stench of greasy fries hits me as the door
opens. I glimpse Dylan and Taylor at a table in the
back, and I can't help checking my hair in my door-
glass reflection. My hair's okay. But what surprises
me is how happy and regular I look, like everybody
else here, as if the only thing in life we need to
worry about is beating the Wildcats next time.
I look away.

Tyrone's on my heels. Right as we step inside,
he snakes his arm around my shoulders. I start to
shove it off, but Dylan waves, as if he's just spotted
me. So I leave Tyrone's arm and wave back.

We take one of the two empty tables left, a table
for two shoved next to a booth that's full of sopho-
mores blowing straws at each other, while poor
Laurie the Waitress tries to write down their orders.

Tyrone gets up. "What do you want?"

"Diet Coke?"

He nods and elbows through people to get to the
counter and call out his order.

I watch him, wondering how I'd describe Tyrone
Larson if I ever needed to—like for a blind date, or
maybe a police lineup. The guy is the epitome of
average. Average height, average weight, average

build. Even his hair is average, brown and unre-
markable. He's not ugly, and he's not handsome.
His clothes are neutral, too. Nine times out of 10,
he'll be dressed just like he is tonight—jeans and a
plain slogan-less T-shirt.

I don't know if it's worse sitting here by myself
or with Tyrone. Summoning up my cheerleader
smile, I check out the room. Dylan and Taylor are
eating fries. Megan and Hale aren't here yet. Sammy
and the team haven't made it over yet, either. I'm
already glancing at the clock on the wall, trying to
figure how soon is too soon to leave.

Tyrone plunks my Coke in front of me and
scoots his chair around so we're sitting closer than
across the table. He has a paper-wrapped sandwich
and a large milk shake.

We have about as much to say to each other
as D.J. and I do. Actually, Tyrone doesn't talk
much more than D.J., but for different reasons.
I always have the feeling that there's not a whole
lot going on in D.J.'s head, and that's why he's not
talkative.

But with Tyrone, it's like he has too much going
on in his brain, like his brain is swirling with sci-
ence theories mere mortals could never understand.
So he's fine not talking unless somebody comes up
with a subject worth talking about.

But I don't want to be seen not having a good
time, so I force myself. "What did you think of tryouts? You had the best view of them. How did you
get out of your gym class anyway?"

Tyrone doesn't bother answering any of my

half hearted questions. Instead he poses one of his own. "What do you think of Mitch?"

It takes me by surprise. It seems like months ago that Mitchell Wade blew into this very place and mesmerized us.

"He's okay." *I can be close-lipped, too, Tyrone, when I want to be.*

I glance over my shoulder at Dylan. He and Taylor are laughing so hard she's dabbing her eyes with a napkin.

"He's got something, doesn't he?" Tyrone throws in.

I swing back around. "What?"

"Dylan Gray." Tyrone takes a big bite out of his fish sandwich.

"Yes, he does. He knows what he believes in."

"Funny," Tyrone says. "You go to church. My dad and I used to. We should know what we believe in, too."

It's no secret that Tyrone's father used to be an officer in some religious, feed-the-starving-kids organization, until he was convicted of fraud. No wonder Tyrone doesn't go to church anymore. Dylan and Tyrone have gotten into some pretty heated discussions about God and Christianity over the years. Some of those discussions have gone on in classes.

"That religious stuff just doesn't work for me anymore," Tyrone says.

"That *religious stuff* works for Dylan, in case you haven't noticed," I counter.

"And Kyra James believes all the things she learned in Sunday school?"

It feels too weird to be talking to Tyrone Larson about God when I do everything I can to avoid the subject with Dylan.

He grins, a skeptical grin.

"Okay," I admit. "So I don't exactly *live the life*, not like Dylan does." A wave of guilt crashes over me. I see myself opening the medicine cabinet, shaking out the pills. I have no business preaching to Tyrone. Maybe I don't know what I believe. But maybe I do. And maybe I'm fighting it, just like Tyrone.

Then Tyrone tells me this long story about his chemistry teacher. I wonder what the point of it is. Then I realize that he's saying that teacher is the one who made chemistry interesting to him . . . something I can't imagine.

"So it's not chemistry that's at fault," I say, "for boring us all to death. It's the person talking about chemistry?"

He puts down the sandwich and stares at me, his eyes hard brown beads. "Yeah, you could say that."

"So maybe it's like that with faith. Like maybe you just listened to the wrong people talk about faith, but faith is still cool."

Tyrone's eyes now look like steel. "Tell you what. Let's go."

"Fine," I say quietly, wondering again why I'm even bothering to talk to Tyrone Larson about God. I must be more tired than I thought. "I think I want to go home."

He gets up, takes the rest of his sandwich, fries, and the shake he hasn't touched, and stuffs them into the trash cans by the door.

I get up and follow him, slipping into my jacket on the way. I say bye to kids who holler after us, asking why we're leaving already.

Tyrone doesn't bother to answer them at all. But at the door he whispers, "Wave good-bye to Dylan . . . if he even looks up from his fun time with Taylor."

I jerk open the door and storm outside. If I had real clothes on, I would keep on walking, all the way home. Instead I turn down the sidewalk toward Tyrone's car. And that's when I see Hale Ramsey strolling toward us with Brianna hanging on his arm. Brianna!

"Where's Megan?" I shout. A frost cloud puffs from my mouth, and I can almost see my question hanging in it.

Hale shrugs, and I know he's dumped Megan for Brianna.

I push past them toward Tyrone's car and get there first. I'm so mad I'm not even cold as I wait for Tyrone to unlock the door. When he does, I slide in, shivering on the cold vinyl seat.

As soon as Tyrone gets in and closes the door, I want to tell him off. Hale Ramsey is a jerk, and so is Tyrone Larson. And so am I for even being here with him.

He starts the car, and I can't read his face. It's carved in stone. But I'm adding up two and two, and I don't like what I'm coming out with. Hale never intended to keep his date with Megan. He didn't need a ride. *I* did. He just wanted to cancel my ride so his buddy Tyrone could come along and save the day. It wouldn't surprise me if Brianna had been in on it all along.

The whole thing was a setup, probably schemed by Tyrone. I should have known. Maybe I did, at least in a way. I sure hadn't fallen for Hale's shyness routine. But all I could think about was myself, getting me a ride. I had to know Megan was asking for trouble buying into Hale Ramsey. But I didn't do anything to stop it, and now Megan would be crushed.

I study Tyrone's profile. Is he smug? Satisfied? He got what he wanted. Here I am, riding in his car. He has to be the King of Selfish.

And what about me? Maybe I'm more like Tyrone than I want to admit. I'm definitely more like him than Dylan. Or Taylor.

Suddenly the last place I want to go is home. If I do go home, I'll feel like I have to call Megan. And I don't know if I can handle any more guilt. My parents will be home, watching TV. I'll have to pretend things are great, make up some excuse why I'm home early. They'll want to know all about the game and how Sammy did.

And there won't be any way to get to their bathroom and get the help I need to calm down, to sleep. And I do need help.

"Tyrone?" I feel like I'm on top of a hill, rolling down, tired of trying to stop myself. "Didn't you say you have a six-pack in the trunk?"

Tyrone doesn't even act surprised. We don't speak as he drives back to school, unless you count my gasps as Tyrone runs a stop sign and accelerates around corners. He takes the gravel road to a spot behind the football field. It doesn't take us long to polish off the six-pack. He even shares 50/50 with me. The beer is icy and gets better with each can.

We don't speak until we're finished.

Then I tell him I want to walk home, and I get out of the car. Even the chilly air doesn't clear the fog in my brain from the three cans of beer.

When I see our house, I take my time walking up the sidewalk. Our outside light is the kind that comes on automatically in case we forget to turn it on. The living-room shades are drawn, but TV light glows and casts shadows through the cracks between slats.

The Grays have turned their porch light off, so I know Dylan's home. Then I see his car in the drive. An owl hoots from somewhere, and I stop and listen to it, the deep, melancholy whistle reaching inside me.

I remember a night one of those summers when our families shared a cabin in Michigan. While everyone else was asleep, Dylan and I sneaked outside in search of the owl we kept hearing all week. We trekked all around the lake and fields. When we got back, burrs sticking to us, along with what would turn out to be poison ivy, we ended up in huge trouble. But it had been worth it.

I reach down now and grab a handful of gravel, then tiptoe to their side of the house, just below Dylan's bedroom window. "Dylan!" I whisper-shout. I toss the smallest bits of rock at the window. They hit dead center. "Yeah!" I'm a great shot!

Taking the biggest rock, I hurl it and miss the

windowpane. But the rock thumps the wall. The window opens, and Dylan, in striped pajamas, leans out.

"Dylan! Come out and play!"

He rubs his eyes. His head disappears, then reappears with glasses. "Kyra?"

"I want to find an owl! Let's go fishing, Dylan!"

"Shhhh! I'll be right down."

The owl hoots again. Across the street, a light goes on. I shift my weight and rub my hands together, watching my breath come out like smoke signals.

The Grays' door opens, and I run to meet Dylan. He's wearing jeans now and a letter jacket over his pajama top.

"What's wrong, Kyra?"

I stumble trying to get to him and catch myself on his shoulders. It strikes me as funny. "Why does anything have to be wrong? You're my buddy, Dylan! Can't buddies go fishing together?"

"Not generally at this hour, in this weather." He sniffs. "You smell like a brewery, Kyra. Shouldn't you go home and sleep it off?"

Tears trickle down my cheeks. I touch them, surprised. "I don't want to smell like beer, Dylan. I don't want to go home—not yet. Please? Can't we talk? Like old times?"

"We'll wake Bethany."

I take his hand and pull him toward the driveway. "Let's fish, Dylan!"

His hand goes to his neck, and he gazes at the sky that glitters with tiny star dots. Sighing, he pulls his hand from mine. "I'll get my keys."

I do a Dylan cheer on the front step until he comes out again. He's carrying a long coat that I gratefully wriggle into, though my hands won't come out of the sleeves. I start giggling and can't stop.

■   ■   ■

Before I know it, we're pulling off the road by McCray's pasture. Dylan helps me out of the car and leads me down the hill to the pond.

"Dylan!" I exclaim when we stop at the edge of the water. "It's beautiful!" Moonlight paints shadows on the white frozen pond. Black branches stretch gnarled fingers to the sky like old men lifting their hands to pray.

"You're crying." Dylan flips over the silver row-boat into the snowy brush. We get in and sit onshore, a foot from the ice. "I'm afraid I'm not prepared for ice fishing," he says. "This will have to do."

Moonlight splashes his profile. Dylan's face is so calm—not harsh, not judging me. But I feel shame like a sponge in my chest, soaking up everything else I was feeling. "I'm sorry, Dylan."

"It's okay. Probably a good idea to sober up before you go home anyhow. What happened to you, Kyra? Where'd you go after the Tiger Den?"

I don't want to tell him. I want him to know, to understand, without making me tell him.

"Dylan, what did you mean that day in the car when you said you didn't know me very well any-more?" More than anything, I want him to know me. I need someone to know me. Right in this pond, we used to fish, swim, tell secrets. I want to do that again, to be *that* Kyra again.

He takes off his glasses and tries to wipe the frost or fog from the lenses. "Remember Sammy's onion theory?"

I shake my head. But I remember something.

"He used to say people were layered, like onions. Friends peel off layers for each other, letting you in deeper and deeper—even if tears are part of the deal."

I do remember now. "Sammy thought we were fives, right? Miranda, you, me, Sammy?"

Dylan nods. "You've moved back up to Layer One and Two, Kyra. That's what I meant by not knowing you anymore. Something's going on inside you, and it scares me. I think it's why you went out with Tyrone, why you got drunk tonight."

My head hurts. I don't feel drunk any longer. I feel sick, seasick. And I don't want to talk about this. "I want to go home, Dylan. Take me home."

Saturday I sleep in until noon and wake up with a killer headache. I make myself work on homework most of the afternoon and then practice my lines.

D.J.'s 20 minutes late picking me up for our big date. By the time he honks for me, I'm ready, but I'm angry. Snow is melting. The night's still cool, but nothing compared to me as I fasten my seat belt.

D.J. starts the car and pulls away from the curb. "It's about a half hour from here." He turns on the radio.

"What is?" I ask sharply.

"Huh?" He makes a sloppy turn onto the highway as he dials for a ball game. "Eric's apartment. You said you wanted to party, right?"

"I thought you meant a birthday party." I'm being sarcastic, but from the confused look on D.J.'s face, he doesn't get it.

"It's not Eric's birthday or anything," he explains.

I sink back against the vinyl seat. The guy's not even fun to argue with.

Outside the window I can make out the Big Dipper and Orion. If Dylan were here, I'd point them out. But with D.J. I might have to explain too much. Or he might try to look out the window, and we'd end up in the ditch.

Even the thought of Dylan embarrasses me. Every time I try to remember last night, I vow to hide from Dylan Gray for the rest of my life. Maybe I'll hide from everybody. Including me.

D.J. speeds, but this still feels like a long drive. Finally he swerves into a gravel parking lot behind an old, brick, two-story complex of maybe 10 or 12 apartments. Music blares from one end of the building.

A fire escape leads to the second story, and we take that, instead of going to the door. The stairs clang and bang as we climb. On the tiny balcony and spilling over to the fire escape are a dozen people, most of them holding beer cans. I recognize Brent, Tressa, Brianna, and a few others.

Manny hollers down at us. "Hey! 'Bout time!"

At the top of the stairs, we thread through couples. The smell of spilled beer and stale cigarettes gets stronger. Most of the couples look closer to Eric's age than ours.

At the back door of the apartment, Tyrone steps

out and raises his beer to me in a silent toast. He's dressed totally in black and is standing by himself. I act like I don't see him.

I know where Tyrone is. Hale can't be far behind. And sure enough, there's Hale Ramsey, standing so close to Brianna she has to be able to smell his bad breath. Makes me shudder.

The stench of pot comes from somewhere. It's okay. I know where to draw the line. I've been to parties. When I was a sophomore, I'd go and not even take a beer. Last year I could nurse one beer the whole night, no matter who else was partying or how many beers they had. I can handle myself.

Miranda waves from the couch. "Kyra!" She scoots away from some girl I've never seen and points to the couch cushion. "I tried calling you all day!"

I sit on the couch, which is about as comfortable as a medium-sized brick. Miranda hasn't gone to many parties I know about. "Are you here with Ryan?" I have to shout over the banging, thumping music.

As if I've summoned him, Ryan appears and hands Miranda a beer. I could get up and give him my seat or go find D.J., but I don't.

Miranda takes the beer and starts telling me about her mom's boyfriend. Ryan fades away.

I nod as she talks, but I'm observing several mini-scenes play out around the room. Two girls are arguing. One guy's getting the brush-off. Hale looks like he's whispering in Brianna's ear.

"How about *your* mom?" Miranda asks. She takes

a sip of the beer, and I wonder if she's drinking or nursing.

"What can I say? I hear you, Miranda." I'm not sure what she's been saying. And I'm not sure why I don't confide in her more. I know at school kids think I have lots of friends. But I don't confide in anybody, so maybe I don't have any friends, not really. Layer One. Sometimes I watch the kids labeled *geeks*. They may only hang out in groups of two or three. But I'll bet *they* have friends, best friends they confide in.

And Bethany. I'd like to be Bethie for a day. She and her buddies in the multi-handicapped unit wear whatever they want, say whatever they want. They light up when they see each other. When Bethany played Special Olympics basketball, opposing teams cheered for both sides. The whole floor, plus the entire bleachers, broke into cheers whenever any one of the kids scored. It's a world I wonder about—where surface layers don't matter and people cheer for more than what they can see.

Miranda leans in and spills her beer—on the couch, not me. "You know, *we* need to have a party like this. If I just knew which nights Shelby would be staying out, that would be so cool!"

"Good idea!" I shout back. The music vibrates the coffee table. I like rock okay, but this noise sounds like somebody drained the music out of it.

D.J. comes out of the kitchen and hands me a beer. He's holding a malt liquor, which he slugs back. Then he shakes the can, verifying that it is indeed empty. "Be back," he mutters.

"Terrific. D.J.'s a bad enough driver sober!" I shout to Miranda. "Good thing Sammy taught me how to use a stick shift because I have a feeling I'll be driving myself home." I set down the beer. At least I have an excuse for not drinking the stuff now.

Nothing happens at the *party* for the next half hour. Nobody dances. I don't meet a single person. D.J. keeps disappearing to talk with his brother, whom I still haven't met. Ryan hangs around us more than D.J. does, but Miranda and I spend most of the time by ourselves on the torture-couch. The higher people get, the funnier they *think* they are, and the harder it is to be around them. It feels like going to war without a gun.

When I'm so bored I'm ready to walk home, D.J. comes over. "My brother wants to meet you."

I shrug to Miranda, then get up and follow D.J. through the living room. It's hard not to step on people. Somebody's passed out in the corner.

Eric's by himself in the bedroom, sitting on the only corner of the bed that doesn't have jackets and sweaters piled on it.

"This is Kyra," D.J. says for this formal introduction.

Eric stands up and puts out his cigarette in the ashtray on the dresser. The cigarette butt joins a dozen others, all deformed, bent, and used. My eyes water from secondhand smoke.

I try to see the family resemblance between the brothers, but it's not apparent. Eric's face is chiseled, his cheeks sallow and sunken. Jagged red lines divide the whites of his eyes, as if his eyeballs have cracked. He's shorter than D.J. and seems shorter yet because of the way he carries himself, slumped.

He nods to D.J., and D.J. turns to leave.

A wave of panic hits me, then fades. What could Eric do in a houseful of people?

Still, I don't like being here. Everybody else is on the other side of the apartment. "Well," I say, smiling, but stepping back, like I'm going after D.J., "nice to meet you . . . Eric."

"No, wait a minute!" He glances behind me and then opens the dresser drawer. "I want to show you something."

"What?" But what I want to ask is *why*, as in *why me?*

He chuckles. "Hey, you're not scared of me, are you?"

I chuckle back. "You and D.J. are pretty scary all right."

His expression changes to surprise. And approval. Like when you don't expect somebody to say something clever, but they do. "I like you, Kyra. I think I can trust you."

I shrug.

"Come on over here and check out what I got hold of." He motions me closer to the open dresser drawer. "I've got a feeling a classy girl like you isn't into weed. You probably don't even like the taste of beer—or the calories, right?"

Inside, something's telling me to get out now. I don't have to stay here. Eric is giving me the creeps.

But I'm curious. If I don't look in the drawer, I'll

be up all night, wondering what's in it. I take a step closer. Then another.

Inside the drawer are bottles of pills, maybe 25 or 30 bottles—all shapes and sizes, all with hand-written labels.

"I can get you anything you need, Kyra. I'll give you a good deal."

There are orange bottles like Mom's. Vials, a couple of small boxes, chubby white bottles. And in the middle is a row of tiny clear bottles of orange pills. Their handwritten, penciled labels read *OxyContin*. The same pill I got from Mitch in his office.

"So?" Eric asks.

I shake my head and back out of the bedroom. I don't stop in the kitchen. Tripping over bodies sprawled out on the floor, I keep going until I find D.J.

"I want to go now," I tell him.

He's listening to an older guy, who seems to be in the middle of a story.

I grab D.J.'s arm and pull him toward the door.

"Wh-what's time . . . what time is it?" His words slur.

"Midnight, D.J.," I lie. "You're going to make me miss my curfew!" It's barely 10:30, but he's so wasted, he doesn't know the difference.

In the parking lot, I pat his pocket for his keys and find them first try. He doesn't even react when I reach in and take the key ring.

I guide D.J. to the passenger side and unlock the door. "There you go, big guy."

"Hey! What you doing?"

I run to the driver's seat and get in. "I have always wanted to drive this car, D.J. You promised I could tonight." The motor starts first try.

"I did?"

And I'm off.

It takes me longer to do the drive than it took D.J. When I pull up a block from home, beside the cornfield, he's snoring, mouth open, his head tilted back on the headrest. I drop the keys into the ashtray, figuring he'll have to be fairly sober to find them. Then I slip out and run home.

■　　■　　■

"Sammy, is that you?" Dad calls from the living room.

"Nope!" I holler, taking off my shoes at the door but leaving my jacket on. The warmth of the house makes me want to melt.

"Kyra? You're home early!" Dad shouts.

"Come on in, honey!" Mom hollers. "Everything all right?"

Dad's reclining in the easy chair. Mom's on the couch, with newspapers spread all around. She's probably checking out real-estate ads.

"Did you have a good time?" Mom asks.

"Yeah." I yawn. "I'm pretty tired. Long day. Think I'll go straight to bed."

"Congratulations again on those tryouts," Dad says. "We can't wait to see you in Shakespeare. I knew you'd get the lead. Sammy's the one I can't believe. Sammy in Shakespeare! Still can't get over that one."

"You should watch this movie with us, Kyra," Mom says, setting down her newspaper and staring at the two talking heads on the TV screen.

"Maybe another time. Thanks. I'm going to bed."

I trudge up the stairs, feeling new aches with every step. My neck's stiff, my eyes hurt, and my stomach feels like I swallowed grease. I could use a couple of Zanax, but there's no way I'll brave it with my parents right downstairs.

And I want to stop taking the pills. I really do. So maybe it's for the best.

But I still haven't forgotten the way a tiny pill can hold off the world, lifting up homework, tests, the play, guys, parents, then flicking them all away like dust. And as I wrestle with my covers and twist in bed before finally dropping off to a fitful night's sleep, my next-to-last thought is of the white pill with the line down the middle.

And my last thought is of the orange pill I got from Mitch that day in his office and the ones I saw in Eric's drawer tonight.

22

At school on Monday, Dylan and I don't talk about the party or our boat ride or onion layers or anything else. I dodge him for a few days. But when we're together for play practice, he's so normal, so *Dylan*, that I put that night out of my head.

■　■　■

The next couple of weeks are crazy. Between cheer-leading practice, play practice, games, and parties, I'm so tired it's all I can do to stay awake in classes.

When I'm not studying and working on papers, I'm memorizing my lines for the play. Mitch jokes around with us at practices, but he makes it clear that he's counting on us. He believes in us, that we'll put on a professional performance.

After the third week of rehearsals, Mitch asks me to stay late. I know I've had a bad practice. I felt so tight, so stiff while we ran through the last scene over and over that I got worse and worse.

"Am I doing something wrong?" I ask after everybody else clears out.

We sit down on the edge of the stage. The rest of the gym is dark. School is more silent than I've ever heard it, like a silent scream.

If Mitch says I'm lousy, that he's disappointed in me, I don't think I can handle it.

"Kyra." His voice is soft. "I just want you to know I think you're doing a great job."

I grip the edge of the stage. I'm so relieved. There's nothing he could have said that would have made me happier. "Thanks," I mutter.

"Do you know why you're such a good actress?"

He thinks I'm a good actress. I shake my head, afraid to look at him.

"It's because, when you're at your best, you're able to lose yourself in Rosalind. You become Rosalind, and there's no more Kyra."

No more Kyra.

"That's when you're at your best."

I glance at him. This is the catch. "When I'm at my best?" I repeat. "What about when I'm *not* at my best?"

He sucks in his breath and lets it out slowly. "Then it shows."

"What shows?"

"Everything. Every worry and childish anxiety that eats up your talent and your energy." He turns and stares at me. "You need to loosen up, Kyra. You can't let that tension spoil your performance." He gives me his warmest smile, better than we get in class. "You're the whole show here. Miranda does an all right job, but she moves with all the grace of a rhinoceros. People will be watching you, Kyra. I need you."

■　■　■

For the next weeks, I work even harder. But as the play date gets closer, I get more and more tense. I'm still trying to limit myself to one Zanax a day, but sometimes, most of the time, I have to have two.

Some days go by on their own without any help from me. I feel like I'm on a moving sidewalk, like they have at the airport. I keep going, passing people. But I'm not on the same land they're on. I move from class to class, do what I'm supposed to do, be what everybody expects, but it's like I'm not there. Like Mitch said . . . no Kyra James here.

Almost every weekend, we crash somebody's house when their parents are out. The parties just kind of happen. As soon as parents leave town, word gets around faster than gossip. We all just drift in— well, almost all. Everybody who is anybody, except Sammy. And pretty soon there's a party.

As You Like It is actually coming along. Everybody has the lines memorized now, so Mitch spends more time blocking and giving us the emotions of the lines. I'm thinking it will be the best play Macon High has ever put on. Even Sammy has turned into a decent actor. And Dylan is the only one of the guys who can pull off the British accent, even though I've never heard Mitch compliment him on it.

■   ■   ■

The weekend before the opening of *As You Like It*, D.J. and I double with Miranda and Ryan to a party at Brent's house.

"Man, these are the coolest wheels in town, D.J.!" Ryan leans over the seat and quizzes D.J. on all the buttons and dashboard stuff.

I turn back to Miranda, who is wisely seat-belted behind me. "So, Miranda, you ready for opening night?"

"Don't even talk about it. I get sick every time I think of it."

I laugh. "You'll do great. You and Sammy are both awesome."

"I'll just be glad to have it over with." She brightens. "I think I'm cool to have the party after the play. Shelby should be gone all night. Can't believe how perfect the timing is!"

I wonder if part of her doesn't think the timing is so perfect. I know my mom wouldn't miss the play if she had smallpox.

D.J. has trouble finding Brent's, so everybody is already there when we walk in. It's a two-story house, with jonquils lining the sidewalk, the first flowers of spring. It hasn't seemed much like spring though. Winter is holding on with both hands and all her fingernails. Still, grass is starting to green, and the air smells fresher. I try to soak it in, but it only makes me feel guilty for walking through most days without noticing nature. I used to watch for the signs of changing seasons.

A lot of kids say hi as we shove our way in. Already the party has the same feel as the others, except the music's better.

Brent shows us where to toss our jackets. "So," he says, "one last fling before the big opening night?"

"Stop it, Brent!" Miranda pleads.

Brent's good in the play, and he knows it. "Kyra," he says, when we're on our way back to the living room, "you gotta talk Sam into coming to some of these parties."

"Tell me about it. I gave up on getting Sammy into the mainstream a long time ago. I'm the last person who could talk him into partying."

"Well, he'll *have* to come to *my* party," Miranda insists. "He better!"

I think I recognize a couple of older guys from Eric's apartment, D.J.'s brother's party. They're sitting with Tyrone and Luke in a corner of the living room.

When I'm halfway through my first beer, Eric walks in like he owns the place. He goes straight to the older guys in the corner and makes them follow him outside. Minutes later, the two guys come back without Eric. But they start working the crowd, moving through and passing out pills to three or four girls.

I get up and walk to the front window to see if Eric's gone. No way am I going to take any of his little samples. But I can't help wondering if he still has those OxyContins. It's been about two months since I had the one Mitch gave me, and I can still remember how it felt.

I'm about to turn away when I see Eric with Hale Ramsey. One of them hands something to the other one. But they're too far away for me to make out anything else.

"What's up?" Miranda asks when I sit back down.

I think about telling her. It has to be something to do with all the drugs at this party. I could tell her that, maybe tell her about me, too—how I had one of Mitch's Oxys, how I haven't been able to shake off the way it made me feel. "Miranda, have you ever felt so stressed you wanted—"

"Kyra!" Brianna stumbles between us on the couch and throws her arms around me. "I'm so happy to see you!" She turns and throws one arm around Miranda. "And you too, Miranda!" She glances from one of us to the other, her eyes glassy, shiny. "You two are so . . . so *beautiful!* Like blonde and brunette! Together!" Her voice cracks, and she starts to cry. "I just love that so much! I love *you guys* so much!"

Over Brianna's head, which is buried in my shoulder, Miranda and I exchange raised-eyebrow looks. Brianna hates both of us, and we all know it.

"That's great, Bri," I say, gently shoving her away. "We're crazy about you, too."

She bounds to her feet. "Did you hear that, everybody? They're crazy about me, too!"

Hale Ramsey slithers in through the front door and shuts the door behind him.

Brianna turns so fast she stumbles. "Hale!" Then, with arms outstretched, she runs across the room toward him.

"Somebody want to tell me what that's all about?" I ask.

"X," Miranda says. "Ecstasy?"

D.J. sits at my feet. "The *love* drug."

"Well, stay away from that one, huh, D.J.?" I've heard kids talk about Ecstasy. Jake, a guy who moved to Macon from the East Coast at the beginning of the year, told us all about rave clubs and Ecstasy. I've heard about the drug at other parties, but this is the first time I've seen it in action.

"I don't know," Miranda says, her voice teasing, "it's a whole new Brianna, and that can't be bad."

■   ■   ■

By the time we leave the party, Brianna is sacked out in the middle of the floor, Hale Ramsey by her side. We step over her to get our jackets. And I'm glad I've never gone that far. In fact, if Mitch is right and everything's relative, I'm not doing all that bad.

The next day, Brianna goes back to hating us.

As the days click off to the play, I feel myself getting more and more uptight and anxious. I'm even worried about dress rehearsal, which Mitch has scheduled for Friday during afternoon classes. Our audience will be the high school and the junior high.

Since the night on the boat when Dylan sobered me up, he and I have been friendly and polite. But I still avoid him when we're not rehearsing. Dylan would say I've crawled back to Layer One.

■   ■   ■

Thursday after school Mitch calls a short practice, our last before dress rehearsal.

We run through the rough spots. Then Mitch gathers us for a pep talk. "Well, we're out of time, people. Between now and tomorrow afternoon, go over your lines. Visualize. Prepare. Then let go. Hang loose!" He fixes me with his gaze, as if the last words are for me alone.

My stomach tenses. I remember everything Mitch has said, that it's up to me, that I'm the show, that I have to loosen up, let go. And sometimes everybody needs a little help.

■ ■ ■

After school, I drive straight home and try to go through the script on my own. But I'm so tired, so exhausted, I can't. I take a Zanax from the buffet—I've been taking from both bottles lately—and go to bed.

■ ■ ■

The next thing I hear is a burst of laughter down-stairs. Sammy and Dad are watching *Scooby-Doo* on cable, which means it's after 5:00.

Furious with myself for oversleeping, I drag out of bed. My thoughts hone in on the little orange bottle in Mom's bathroom and how I could get in there while everybody's home. I can hear Mom's voice downstairs, mixed with Dad's and Sammy's laughter.

Checking the hallway, I slip past Sammy's room, keeping close to the wall. When I reach Mom and

Dad's bedroom, I peek in before pushing the door
farther open. It creaks, but not as loudly as the
squeaky cartoon voices downstairs.

The phone rings. I jump.

Somebody will get it downstairs.

It stops ringing. I'm just about to make my
move, when Mom shouts, "Kyra!"

I pivot and scurry to the top of the stairs.

Mom, still in her black business suit, yells up,
"You're awake? Good. Telephone. It's for you." She
heads back toward the kitchen.

I take a breath, then cross back to my room and
pick up the phone. My hands are shaking. "Hello?"

"You sound groggy. Did I wake you up?" It's
Dylan.

I sit on my bed, the phone in my lap. "Are you
kidding? I'm no slouch."

"Want to work on lines together? I can't believe
dress rehearsal is tomorrow. And I'm having trouble
with Act 3. I could use a little help from a pro."

I'm so grateful to be talking to Dylan again,
grateful he called. "Sure. I can use the practice. I'll
be right over, unless you want to work here—but
I warn you, it's the *Scooby-Doo* hour."

"Here's great. I'm baby-sitting Bethany."

I hear Bethany protest in the background. Then
Dylan corrects himself. "I mean, Bethany and I are
hanging out together over here."

"Got it. I'll be right over."

I pull my hair back in a ponytail and change into
my gray sweats and a green sweatshirt, neither of
which would normally leave these four walls—not on

my body anyway. But Dylan won't mind. He probably won't even notice.

Outside, it's gorgeous. A robin flies off our maple tree when I come out. The air is still chilly, but everything's starting to feel like spring.

I knock on the Grays' front door. It opens, and out runs their scruffy mutt.

Afraid he'll run off, I wheel around and go after him. "Bag! Come here, boy! Here, Doggie Bag!"

Bag circles the yard, then runs to me and pounces. Holding on to his collar, I lead him back to the front door. Doggie Bag jerks away but dashes inside.

I stand up and see Bethany in the doorway. She's wearing a white costume of curlycue wool and tiny, pointed, black ears sticking out of a white hood.

"Don't tell me," I say. "You're lost, and Little Bopeep is looking for you."

Bethany laughs. "No, silly! I'm a lamb."

I rub her soft wool. "You sure are. And the cutest little lamb I've ever seen."

"*I'm* going to be in a play, too!" Bethany glances at her brother, who's just joined us. "Aren't I, Dylan?"

"You sure are!" he says. "My sister, the movie star."

"No, sir," Bethany chides. "Not a movie. A play! For church."

"Cool!" I cross to the big oak dining table and toss my script there.

"I'm one of Jesus' sheep," Bethany explains. "Will you come and see me?"

I turn to face her. "Are you kidding me, Bethany Gray? Would I miss seeing you in a play? Of course, I'll be there! When is it?"

She wrinkles her forehead and turns to Dylan. "You tell her, Dylan."

"Tomorrow night, you goof!"

"You're on! And you better show up for Dylan's and my play, although it will probably be pretty boring compared to yours."

"I'm coming!" Bethany nods so hard, her lamb ears slip down.

"So, do you have all your lines memorized?" I ask.

She nods again. "Wanna hear one?"

"You bet!"

Bethany pulls her hood back up so the ears stand up straight. She clears her throat. *"Baa baa baa."* Then her smile breaks wide open.

I applaud heartily. "That's awesome, Bethie!"

"Yep. Sounds *just* like a horse," Dylan says.

"Dylan!" Bethany and I say simultaneously.

"He's just jealous because he's having trouble memorizing *his* lines," I whisper.

Bethany giggles.

"Speaking of which," Dylan says, plopping his script down next to mine on the oak table, "Kyra and I better get to work, Bethie. This would be the perfect time for you to clean your room, okay?"

Bethany objects, but only a little. Then she trots upstairs, *baa*-ing, her lamb's tail wagging.

I take one of the wooden chairs and scoot up to the table, thinking how different this house is from mine, even though the two buildings have the same layout. Dylan's house is lived-in. I don't mean old, although it could be that our oldest piece of furniture is newer than their newest couch. But it's like the Grays haven't chosen anything in the house just to make it look good or because it's the style.

Their carpet is multi-browns to hide tracked-in dirt. Our carpet is white, and we take our shoes off as soon as we come in from outside. We've divided the entry room from the living room, so that the first thing visitors to our house see is the room we weren't allowed to play in as kids. Not even my parents use the entry room, unless we have company.

The first thing anybody sees when they walk into the Grays' entry is an elephant tree-trunk lamp Dylan and Bethany gave their parents for Christmas a hundred years ago. It's the size of Rhode Island and aggressively ugly. But I love it. And once, when Dylan and I made his parents play our *what-three-things-would-you-take-if-your-house-burned-down* game with us, both Mr. and Mrs. Gray picked the elephant lamp.

You could lose yourself in the Grays' old pillowed couch. Our latest couch is firm and sleek and not all that comfortable, even if we were allowed to sit on it. Even their dining table is friendlier—round instead of edged, and bearing the marks and nicks of kids and family.

Dylan brings me a can of Diet Coke and a grape soda for himself. He sits down with me at the table. "Take it away, pro."

We pick a scene and say our lines to each other.
I choose an earlier scene I have trouble with, and we
do that one, then go back to Act 3. I read as Jaques
when he needs me to, and he takes over Celia's lines
when I need it. Everything about reading with Dylan
is fun—saying the lines, discussing the meanings,
taking breaks with Bethany and Doggie Bag.

But when we get to the part where Rosalind pretends to be the young man, Ganymede, Dylan can't
keep a straight face.

"Stop it, Dylan!" I plead, trying to keep from
laughing myself. "We'll never get through the script
at this rate."

He takes off his glasses and pinches the bridge
of his nose. "Here's the problem, and it's only going
to get worse in dress rehearsal. I'm supposed to
have fallen in love with Rosalind, right?"

"Yeah."

"Only when I talk to you in this scene, you're
pretending to be a young man. And I'm supposed
to believe you're a guy?"

"You got it."

Dylan shakes his head. "How am I supposed to
do that? Pretend *you're* a guy?"

"Hey, *I* have to pretend I'm a guy."

"True. You win," he admits. "Having to pretend
you're a guy, when you are in actuality Kyra James,
that's got to be tough. You have my complete sym-
pathy."

I think about saying, *Dylan, if you only knew*
how easy it is for me to pretend, to act on a daily
basis, you'd really feel sorry for me.

Instead, I turn it into a joke. "That's why they pay me the big bucks, Dylan."

Dylan doesn't laugh. He puts both hands flat on the table and stares at them. He has large hands, rough in a good way. "Kyra, don't bite my head off, okay? But I'm worried about you."

I sit up straighter, anger ignited like a lit match. I know he's going to bring up the time I had too many beers and made him take me out on the boat. Why can't he just let us enjoy the moment, the *now*, as Mitch says?

"Listen, don't take this wrong. I'm not getting down on you. I'm just . . . okay, I'm not exactly in the in group—"

"Obviously. The *in group* hasn't called itself the *in group* since the sixties, Dylan." I hope this can make the joke, get us back to safe ground.

"But even *I* hear things. Not like people are talking about you. Everybody thinks you hung the moon. You know that."

"Hung the moon? Another keen phrase."

He trudges on as if I haven't spoken. "But I know you've been going to D.J. and Eric's parties. And I know some of what goes on there. And you've been acting . . . well, not like yourself lately—"

"I'm *acting*, Dylan. I'm not supposed to be myself. I'm Rosalind." I pick up the script. "Could we get back to that, please?"

The front door opens, and Mrs. Gray walks in, her arms filled with plastic grocery bags. "Hey, kids! Studying?"

"Studying play lines." Dylan gets up and walks

over to her. "Let me get those for you." He takes all
of the bags and carries them into the kitchen.

"Hi, Mrs. Gray," I say, smiling. "Bethany fell
asleep already."

"That's good. I tell you, Kyra, it's so nice to find
you here. Just like old times. We don't see enough
of you anymore. I'm glad you're helping Dylan
with his lines, too. I'll bet you guys will be sad to
have the play end." She glances at Dylan, then grins
sheepishly at me. "You know, I always wanted to be
in a play."

I smile back at her. Totally normal. A normal
conversation. "Even Bethany's been bitten by the
theater bug, huh?" I ask.

She laughs. "Was she still wearing that sheep's
costume?"

Dylan comes back and sits at the table. "Are you
kidding? She wouldn't even take it off to go to bed."

"Good thing that play is tomorrow or we'd have
to make a new costume," she says. "That one already
looks like the lamb's been caught in the briars." But
she doesn't sound mad about it.

Mrs. Gray heads for the kitchen. "How about
something to eat? Dylan's dad should be home
before long. This is his late night at the lumberyard,
so we eat fashionably late. You'll stay, won't you,
Kyra?"

"I better not." Two seconds ago I would have
jumped at the chance to stay here longer. But even
the Grays' house is edgy now. I don't want to give
Dylan another chance to bring up D.J.'s parties.
"Another time? Thanks for asking me."

Dylan and I go back to Act 3. I hear the fridge open and shut, bags rustling, water running.

"That's your cue," Dylan says, pointing to the line.

The phone rings.

"I'll get it!" Mrs. Gray shouts from the kitchen. "Hello?" Her phone voice is the same as her regular voice. "Well, how are you? Do you want to speak to—" There's a pause. "Yes. She's right here. Shall I put her on so—"

Dylan and I stop talking.

"Right now? I was hoping she could stay for dinner. They're right in the middle of—"

There's a short silence. Then Mrs. Gray says, "Of course. I'll tell her. Bye."

When she comes out to the table, her eyebrows are lowered and she looks confused. "Kyra, that was your mother. She wants you to come home."

"Now?" I can't think of any reason she'd make me come home. She knows I'm working on the play.

Mrs. Gray shrugs. "Yes. Right away."

I get up and take my script. Something has to be wrong. Maybe there's been an accident. Dad? Sammy?

"I'm sure nothing's wrong," Mrs. Gray says.

"Want me to walk with you?" Dylan offers.

My hand is already on the doorknob. "No. Thanks. Tell Bethie bye. I'll . . . we can . . . I better go. Thanks. Bye."

The wind kicks up as I run down the sidewalk, cut through the lawns, and race up the steps to my front door.

Mom's waiting for me inside, her arms crossed in front of her.

"What's wrong?"

Before she can answer, Dad marches in, frowning. He's not looking directly at me.

Then I see Sammy, sitting on the entry-room couch, the couch where no one ever sits. He's quiet, his hands clasped loosely at his knees. And I know something is very wrong.

"What is it?" I scream, my mind racing. They're all here. Mom, Dad, Sammy. There couldn't have been an accident. Maybe Sammy's sick. Maybe—

"Take a seat over there by your brother, Kyra," Dad commands. It's a voice I haven't heard in a long time, stern, brusque.

"Will somebody tell me what's going on?" But I do as I'm told and sit beside Sammy.

Sammy doesn't look at me. I can't take this.

Dad moves closer, and Mom stands behind him, both of them looking at our shoes, at the couch armrests, anywhere but at us.

Finally Dad speaks, silencing all of my questions. "I want to know right now who's been taking your mother's pills!"

This is it. *It's all over. They're onto me.* Panic slices through me. I'm not afraid of what they might do to me. I'm terrified of what they'll *think*. I'm their star, their good girl.

The irony is that I need a Zanax at this minute more than I've ever needed one.

Tell them. Tell Mom that you feel pressure that won't go away, not even with her pills. Tell Dad you're sorry you took them, that you're out of control, that you don't know what's happening to you.

But they'd never get over it.

"What pills?" I hear myself ask. I sound calm, amused. Even I don't know how I'm doing this.

"No kidding." Sammy leans forward, on the edge of this couch, where neither one of us has ever sat—

not with our parents home anyway. "Why's Mom taking pills?"

"We'll ask the questions!" Dad snaps.

Sammy jerks back as if he's been slapped.

Dad lowers his voice, but it's being held in by a slender thumb in the dike. I hear it in his tone. "Your mother has a condition—nothing for you to worry about—that requires prescription medication. In the wrong hands, those drugs can be . . . abused. Understand?"

Mom's standing behind him, her arms wrapped around herself as if that's all that's keeping her from shattering into pieces. "Jeff, I told you this wasn't—"

Dad glares back at her. "Linda, let me finish!"

She puts her hand over her mouth. Her cheeks glisten with tears in the bright entry-room light that transforms this guest spot into an interrogation room.

Dad turns back to us. "I'm going to ask you one at a time. And I want you to look me in the eyes and tell me the truth."

"Dad, this—," Sammy starts.

But Dad cuts him off with a glare. Then he turns to me. "Kyra, did you take your mother's pills?"

"You're serious." I picture my own incredulous grin. I'm good. A born actress, like Mitch said.

"I have never been more serious in my life," Dad answers, his eyes darting until he can focus on my face, my eyes.

I picture this as a scene, in a play or a movie. Dad's line fits perfectly, delivered just right.

"Jeff?" Mom cries weakly from stage left.

But this is real. This is hurting them. I can see that. It's my chance to come clean here and now. Wouldn't they help me? Could it be any worse than the way I feel now?

I glance at Mom. "Why would I take your medicine, Mom?"

"Just answer the question, Kyra!" Dad demands.

Slowly, dramatically, I shift my gaze from Mom to Dad. Dad and I stare at each other, and I wonder what he's thinking, what he's remembering. I don't move my eyes while I answer. "I did not take Mom's pills."

He turns to Sammy. "Sammy, tell me the truth. Did you take those pills?"

"Man, Dad!" Sammy shifts on the couch, his hands twisting in his lap. "I can't believe you're asking me this!"

"Just answer me, Sammy." Dad is pleading now.
"No!"

Poor Sammy. I lie better than he tells the truth.

"Because if you did, Son . . . ," Dad says, sitting down on the other side of Sammy. The couch creaks in surprise. "If you did, we can talk about it. I was a teenage boy once, too. I know what goes on, believe me."

Sammy holds his head with both hands. "Dad, I don't do that stuff!"

Dad sighs. The anger has drained out of him, leaving a shell coating that looks as if it could crack into a million pieces. "I'll give you one last chance," he says so softly that Mom steps closer. "Did you take the pills?"

"I—no—man! I didn't. No," Sammy stammers, making him look guiltier.

"Stop it, Jeff!" Mom explodes into tears. "I told you our children wouldn't do this!"

Dad gets up and goes to her, putting his arm around her shoulder. Then he turns back to Sammy, who looks like he might cry, too.

I feel as if I'm not even here.

"Sammy, what about your friends? Maybe one of them—"

"No way!" Sammy protests.

"Jeff," Mom pleads, "we know their friends. They're good kids. It had to be somebody else! Somebody broke in—"

"And left half of the bottle? Didn't take anything else?" Dad lets go of Mom and paces in front of us.

I feel like vomiting. This is all my fault. Sammy's in agony. He has to be able to read our dad well enough to know the suspicion is still there.

Tell them. Tell them the truth.

But that inner voice is getting weaker and weaker, fading into the walls. My parents think I'm perfect. I can't lose that. I have to have someone believe in a good Kyra, even if it's a lie.

"What about the cleaning company?" Mom asks, hope glinting. "They could have done it!"

Dad starts to shake his head. But he sucks his bottom lip, and I can see how much he wants to believe his kids didn't steal pills from his wife. "The cleaning service did have access," he admits. "I guess someone . . . well, they might just take a few, leave the rest, thinking we wouldn't notice. . . ."

"That's it!" Mom's eyes are wide. She's trembling. "I told you, Jeff!"

"Can I go now?" My voice is flat, injured.

"Look, kids. I had to ask. You understand that, right?" Dad's trying to apologize. It's as close as he ever gets.

I get to my feet. So does Sammy. I think I feel the worst for what this is doing to my brother. It's not fair. Wrong. In so many ways.

"Sure. Go on," Dad says, waving his hand like he's flicking flies off food.

Sammy tears up the stairs ahead of me and slams his bedroom door.

Mitch's words surround me as I trod up the stairs. *Sometimes people need a little help.*

I have never needed help more than I do right now. I close the door to my room, pick up my phone, and dial D.J.

He answers. "Yeah?"

"D.J., can you come get me right away? I need to see your brother."

It takes three hours, but I get what I wanted.
D.J. drove me in silence to Eric's apartment. I'd figured a bottle of OxyContin would be expensive, but
not that expensive. I didn't have enough cash. And
Eric wasn't about to take a check. So D.J. took me
to an ATM, where he got cash and let me write him
a check. It was the most creativity I'd ever seen in
him.

Through the clear glass of the tiny bottle with
the black cap, I can count the 15 orange pills in the
bottom. They look like candy.

My mind shuts down on the drive back. If D.J.
says anything, I don't hear him. I shove the bottle
into my purse and promise myself I won't take a single pill until I absolutely have to, to loosen up, to
disappear into the role, like Mitch says.

But even I don't believe my promises anymore.

■ ■ ■

Friday I carry the bottle of Oxys with me to school.

Miranda is waiting for me at my locker. "Dylan's looking for you."

Dylan Gray is the last person I want to see. I close my locker, and we swim upstream to English.

"Hey, Kyra!" Taylor calls as we pass her in the halls. "Dylan's looking for you!"

The pills weigh heavily in my purse, even though the bottle is smaller than my finger. As we make our way through the halls, Miranda bubbles over about having the cast party at her house after the play. "Mitch is even coming!"

In the last week or so, every other word out of her mouth is *Mitch*.

Dylan's head bobs over the crowd at the far end of the hall, and I duck into English class and take a seat in the back row. I wonder what Mitch would think if he knew we had matching pill bottles.

■ ■ ■

I don't even open my purse until after lunch. I have it all timed out so I'll be loose, ready for dress rehearsal.

Heading out of the cafeteria with Miranda and D.J., I put on my brakes. "Oops. Forgot something. You guys go on. I'll catch up with you."

"What did you forget?" Miranda asks.

"My pen."

She laughs. "You leave pens everywhere you go. And pick up others. What's the big deal?"

"Not my pen. I've got to get it back."

Miranda shrugs. D.J. does as he's told and lumbers away.

I go back to our table, making sure Miranda and D.J. are long gone. Then I keep walking, through the double doors, and out to the opposite hall. Before I get to the water fountain, I take the bottle out of my purse and clutch it in one hand.

When I'm sure nobody's looking, I twist the cap and shake out one OxyContin into my palm. I shift the bottle to my left hand, put the pill in my mouth, and lean down for a long drink.

"Kyra, what are you doing?" Dylan's standing behind me.

I jerk up, spilling water on my shirt. "Scare the life out of me, why don't you!" The pill is stuck in my throat, making me swallow. The taste is bitter. Inside my fist the bottle still feels cold.

"Answer me, Kyra," Dylan says evenly. "What did you just take?"

"None of your business!" I snap. "Why are you following me?"

"I'm not. You left so suddenly last night after your mom called, I was afraid something was wrong. I tried to call you, but your mother said you were out."

"Nothing's wrong," I lie. "Mom just pulled one of her panic routines." I turn my back on him and shove the bottle into my purse.

"Okay." He's so calm I want to scream. "Maybe

there's nothing wrong with your mom. But something's wrong here, Kyra. I saw you taking something from—"

"Did you hear me, Dylan? I told you to butt out. This is none of your business!"

"Don't be that way—"

"I *am* that way! Live with it, Dylan! *I* have to. And if I need something to help me live with it, then that's my business. Get it?"

"You don't need that, Kyra."

I see myself in his glasses, as if I'm far, far away from his eyes. "You don't have any idea what I need."

"I know you well enough to know you don't need those."

"You don't know me!" I'm mocking him, remembering. "I'm Layer One all the way. *I* don't even know me. Nobody does! But do you want to know something, Dylan? When I take this—" I point to my purse, to the pills waiting inside—"I don't care. I don't care! Do you have any idea what a relief it is not to care? I spend my whole life caring what everybody thinks! So sometimes I need a little help."

"Everybody needs help, Kyra. Just not from a pill."

I know he's talking about Jesus and God, and it makes me even angrier. If Jesus and God came in a bottle, maybe I *would* take them.

"Leave me alone, Dylan!" I shout. "Just leave me alone!"

One of the junior high teachers sticks her head out of her room. "Hey! Quiet down and get to class!"

degrees of guilt

I turn and run down the hall and duck into the bathroom. Nobody's there, and my footsteps echo on the cold floor. My sobs bounce off bare walls. I dash to the last stall, lock the door, and sink to the floor, hugging my knees.

One of the toilets is dripping. The *plink, plink* grows louder and louder, drowning out everything else. It sounds like music, calming, steady. I can feel myself disappearing, fading, drifting farther and farther away, like I was in Dylan's glasses, no more than a speck.

I'm missing class. I'm missing class, and I don't care. *I,* Kyra James, do not care. It's almost funny. I laugh and then cover my mouth.

I don't move until the door to the bathroom swings open and footsteps clamor in with high-pitched voices. I come out and see freshmen girls lining up for stalls and a place at the sink.

"Hey! Look! You're in the play, aren't you?"

"That's Kyra James, idiot. She's the star of the play."

I smile at them. I feel like a star. They step aside so I can put on lipstick and brush my hair. They watch me as if they'll have a test on me later.

My head feels like it's floating as I move toward the door. "See you in the gym, girls!"

They call good luck after me as I stroll to the gym.

"Kyra! Where have you been?" Brent shouts as I float down the rows of chairs toward the stage.

"Mr. Purdy asked about you in computers," Miranda says. She's wearing her costume. "You okay?"

"Never better!" I shout.

"What's with you, Kyra?" Sammy asks, frowning at me.

"I am no longer Kyra," I announce. "I am Rosalind!"

"Well, Rosalind," Mitch says, grinning at me, "you better get your costume on."

I run backstage to the changing room and get dressed. When I come out, the stage is filled with Elizabethan costumes, and I feel like I'm in England.

Dylan stares at me as I walk out. He starts toward me, but I run to Mitch.

"I can't wait to act!" I exclaim.

Mitch smiles and puts his hands on my shoulders and shakes them a little. "You are definitely loose. Good for you!"

I *am* loose. And when the curtain goes up, I'm so eager to get on the stage that I rush my entrance and come out too early.

We move through the first act as if we're all dreaming the same dream.

Three or four times I forget my lines. But it doesn't matter. I don't care. *I'm* Rosalind. So I say whatever I feel like saying. Miranda is thrown off and stumbles over words, as if trying to remember where the script says that. The audience laughs, and I turn and laugh with them. But Dylan goes with it, saying his lines and, I think, half of mine.

And I feel as if I'm on the ceiling, watching all of us.

When I exit stage left, Brent's there waiting. "Are you okay, Kyra?"

"I'm wonderful!" I answer, walking past him. I need water. I don't think I've ever been this thirsty.

"She's higher than a kite," Brent mutters to somebody.

But I don't care what they say. I honestly don't care. Zanax makes things not matter. These pills make me not care. And that feels so good.

■   ■   ■

By the fourth act, my head is buzzing. I'm not floating anymore. Each line costs me. My brain is foggy, and I have to be cued over and over again.

And I care.

I can see in the faces of the kids in the front row that they're bored. Or worse. Chairs squeak. Someone is popping gum. Teachers lean out of their seats to get kids to stop whispering. I think about the girls in the john, how excited they'd been to see me in the play. What are they thinking now? What do they think of their *star* now?

When the play ends and the curtain closes
for the last time, all applause is mandatory and
underclassmen don't complain about going back
to their classes.

Behind the curtain, the players shuffle, picking
up props, finding their scripts. We know it was
lousy. We know why.

"Good job, people," Mitch says without enthusiasm. "Now we know the rough edges we need to file
off by tomorrow night, right? Everybody study those
scripts. And loosen up!"

Mitch keeps talking, but I can't hear him. All
I hear is the roar in my ears. It's so loud I expect
everyone to turn to see what the ruckus is about.

But nobody's looking at me. Even Miranda and
Sammy avoid eye contact.

I move behind the stage curtain, all the way to

the back, by the fire exit, where I slide to the floor and put my head on my knees. I cover my ears and try to make the roaring stop.

When it does, I look up and am shocked that I'm the only one left onstage. They're all gone—audience, players—everybody.

"I'll drive you home, Kyra." Dylan's behind me, a couple of feet away, leaning against the cooler.

I don't look at Dylan as he guides me through the cafeteria exit and out to his car. "I just want to sleep. I'll be all right if I get some sleep."

On the way home I guess I doze off in spurts of time interspersed with flashes of light and window scenery. Images come and go like a bad videotape. I need tracking. I see Dylan—then I don't. Then I do, and he's gripping the steering wheel, praying—I know it. And I wish I could hear that, what Dylan's saying to God and what God's saying back.

And then I'm home.

Nobody's there, and Dylan walks me up the stairs to my room. Falling into my bed feels like descending into a deep hole, black and bottomless. I feel Dylan take off my shoes. Then he pulls the blanket over me because I'm shivering.

The light goes out. Footsteps fade. And I'm falling asleep and hoping I'll never wake up.

■   ■   ■

"Kyra? Are you still asleep? You've got to get ready!" Sammy's voice comes through cotton to get to me.

I open my eyes, but it's hard. My eyelids are

weighted. I look down at my ruffled sleeves, the red satin costume gown, and try to remember where I am and what happened. When it comes to me, the rehearsal, the fool I made of myself, I lie down again, pull the covers over my head, and curl into fetal position.

"I can't believe you slept in your costume." Sammy chuckles, like it's a joke, like things can ever be normal again. "You better hurry up and get dressed. Mom and Dad are leaving right now."

I don't understand. I won't go to school. And I don't care when my parents leave.

"Kyra! Sammy!" Mom yells from downstairs. "We are absolutely leaving right this minute! You can come now or drive yourselves."

I make myself sit up and look out the window. It's a gray-dark, smoky dusk. "Where are they going? It's too early for school."

"School?" Now Sammy really laughs. "Kyra, it's not morning. Did you forget about Bethany's play at church?"

"Bethany!" Her play. The lamb costume. How could I have forgotten that?

"Bye!" Dad shouts. The door downstairs slams.

"Guess we're driving ourselves," Sammy says.

I sit on the edge of the bed, too fast, and my head rebels with hammers and scythes. "Just give me a minute to change, Sammy."

"We have to take your car. My pickup's running on fumes."

I stand up. My head feels like those desk wave machines where the water sloshes one way and then the other, tilting the glass frame. "You drive though, okay?"

"Good idea."

■ ■ ■

In the car, Sammy keeps giving me side-glances. "Are you okay, Sis?"

"I'm swell. Don't I look okay?"

"You look fine. Kind of a rough afternoon though."

I must have been as awful as I think I was, or Sammy wouldn't have said anything. "Don't worry about it. I'll be magic tomorrow." I grin at him and think how handsome he's gotten while I wasn't looking. It shocks me to see this, as much as if we hadn't been together for the last five years.

I don't want to let Sammy down tomorrow night, or my parents or Dylan . . . or Mitch. Mitch, maybe more than anyone else, is counting on me.

I know what I need to do. I don't like what the Oxy pill did to me. But it was okay until it wore off and left me stranded alone on that stage. I'll need to take a second pill, between acts, before the first one wears off. And after that, no more.

But I have to get through tomorrow. *Sometimes everybody needs a little help.*

■ ■ ■

As soon as we get to church, we hurry to the Grays' row. They've saved us seats in the first pew. Mr. Gray has his video camera running already.

Mrs. Gray reaches over and squeezes my hand, as Sammy and I take the end seats, farthest from Dylan. "You made it!" Mrs. Gray exclaims. "Bethany would have been crushed if you hadn't."

The program starts with special numbers and songs from the younger kids. When the sheep file out, with Bethany smack in the middle, Dylan bursts into applause, and Mrs. Gray has to quiet him down.

Bethie looks so cute in her costume. She stands so tall that I think she's on her tiptoes most of the time.

A couple of sheep scenes follow. First, a thief dressed in robes tries to call the sheep. But they won't go to him, and they run when he tries to steal one of the lambs. Another costumed girl tries to do the same thing from stage right, but the sheep are too smart for her. Finally, the sheep huddle together at the front of the stage, and Bethany steps forward. *"Baa, baa, baa."* Her bottom lip is pursed out, and she's trying to look sad.

A boy a head taller than Bethany walks out from stage left and stops in front of her. "What's the matter, little lamb? Are you lost?"

Bethany nods. *"Baa, baa."*

The boy strokes Bethany's furry white head and says, "No, you're not lost! Because I *know* you! And you know me! You're my little lamb!"

He calls the sheep, and this time they circle around him. "You're all my sheep. I'm the gate. Those who come in through me will be saved. Wherever they go, they will find green pastures. The thief's purpose is to steal and kill and destroy.

My purpose is to give life in all its fullness. . . . I am the good shepherd; I know my own sheep, and they know me."

Tears fill my head and leak out. And I envy Bethany and Dylan, who know God like that. I want to be known, to know myself. Layer Ten know. But I'm afraid. *God, I am afraid to let you know me that well, to see down into the depths, where I know I'm ugly and even you can't love me.*

"Sammy," I whisper, "I'm leaving. Come on."

"Huh?" Sammy turns his head. I'm sitting on the wrong side. "Let's go! Now!" I've shouted it, and heads turn to us. I stand up and whisper to Mrs. Gray, "I'm sorry. I have to go. Tell Bethie . . . tell her she was wonderful."

I stumble to the aisle and keep going, ignoring whispers.

"Slow down, Sis," Sammy urges.

I'm stone-cold sober now, so I drive. My car is the first to leave the church lot. I ease my foot off the accelerator.

"You sure you're okay?" Sammy asks. I think he's studying me.

I nod. I can lie without words now.

"Bethany was great, wasn't she?" I can hear Sammy's grin without looking at him. "Cute play."

"Yeah. She was great." But I don't want to think about the play, hers or mine. I don't want to think. And I know only one way to do that. It's sitting in my lap right now, inside my purse.

"You're going too fast," Sammy insists as I reach the cornfield.

I lift my foot from the pedal, turn onto our street, and wonder if my head will ever stop buzzing.

"Kyra, look out!"

I focus and see the face of a young deer, ears up and eyes staring at us. I slam on the brakes.

A shadow blocks the windshield, and I hear a *thud* and a *thump*.

"Sammy!" I scream, swerving, braking, clutching the wheel.

The car stops. I manage to turn just short of the ditch.

"Are you all right?" Sammy pops his seat belt and climbs out. He leans into the car. "Kyra! Are you okay?"

I nod. But I'm not okay. My heart is still racing down the street. I'm empty. Through the rearview mirror, I see Sammy jogging to something beside the road.

I open the door and spill out of it, my purse hitting the pavement as I stumble and race after Sammy.

He's squatting beside a doe—young, fawn-spotted, not moving. There's no blood anywhere. There should be blood when you kill something.

I can't breathe. But I kneel on the other side of the deer and stare at its lifeless body.

I did this.

Guilt presses in on me, seeping into my veins and circulating to all parts of my body. I can't stop tears from falling, but I'm silent as the night. Stars fill the sky, and the moon is a big eye, full and clear—like the eye of God.

"Is he watching, Sammy?" I whisper.

Sammy looks up. He's crying, his hand resting on the doe's back. "Who? Is who watching?"

"God?" I feel Sammy's gaze, but I can't take my eyes off the deer's tiny nose, still glistening wet. "I should have seen it, Sammy. I didn't want to—"

"Kyra, it's not your fault." He's quiet, and I don't think either of us believes him.

We stay like this, bent over the deer, neither of us talking. A bird caws. I hear the flutter of wings. Wind bows the branches above us. I can see the outside light of our house through the mist at the end of the street.

Finally Sammy says, "Yeah, I think God *is* watching. But not the way you mean."

I can see the doe clearly in the moonlight, too clearly. Its eyes are open, deep and expectant. I glance up. Sammy's staring down at me. He's stopped crying, and I can't tell what he's thinking. I can't read my twin's mind, not anymore.

"I've got buddies," he begins softly, "you know, like Tyrone, who doesn't believe much in a God watching us from heaven." Sammy's fingers move to stroke the deer's neck. "And guys like Manny, who are terrified God is watching every move they make."

I don't breathe.

Sammy laughs, soft as moonlight. "But *I'm* glad God sees me all the time, even when I screw up. Just so long as he sees." Sammy squints at me with an intensity I have never seen in him. "What would scare me, Kyra, make *me* jump in front of your car and hug the metal, is if God ever closes his eyes. Then nobody sees me, and I'm not here."

Not there. I digest every word. Sammy has never talked like this. Where did he get thoughts like these? I want to hug him, to cry into him, to soak up his *Sammy-ness.*

He stands up. "I better go see if your car will start."

I watch him jog back to the car, the moon spreading a path for him. I can almost feel God watching both of us—seeing, knowing, caring.

At the driver's door Sammy stoops down and picks something off the ground. Then instead of getting in and starting my car, he turns and walks slowly back. My purse is in one hand. The other hand, he's holding in front of him, palm up, as if he's found a baby bird fallen from a tree and has to be careful with it.

When he's still a few feet away, Sammy looks at me. His eyes scream disappointment, disbelief.

And I know what's in his hand, what he found on the ground.

"Kyra, what *is* this? What are you doing with these?" He storms all the way up to me and shoves the tiny glass bottle under my nose.

"Give me those, Sammy!" I grab for them, but he's too fast for me. "Those aren't yours! Give them back!"

"I can't believe you, Kyra! You know better than this! How could you do it? Why?" He paces in a fast tight circle, like a rabid wild animal. "Where did you get these—?" He stops and studies the bottle. "Are they Mom's?" I've removed the label. Let him think they are Mom's. "Kyra, *you?* You took Mom's drugs?"

I swipe at his hand. "Give it back!"

"And Dad still thinks *I* did it!"

"So what?" I explode. "You *should* take them, Sammy! There's nothing wrong with pills. *Mom* takes them! *You* should take them! Maybe you wouldn't be such a loser." I can't stop. I want the pills back. They're *my* pills.

"They talk about you at parties, Sammy. Sammy the Straight Arrow. You should hear Miranda." I get a reaction from him on that one. I hit home, and I keep hitting. "Yeah, your buddy *Randi.* You won't even go to her party because you're so much better than the rest of us. Is that what you think, Sammy? Well, it's not what Miranda thinks!" I know I'm hurting him, but I can't stop.

I can't see his face now. He's a shadow blocking the moonlight. But the shadow twists and heaves, and I think Sammy's never been this furious in his whole life.

"Miranda would 100 times rather be with Ryan than you. You know why?"

"Stop it, Kyra."

"Because Ryan's at least a little fun! He's not stuck back in sixth grade building snowmen and goofing off."

"That's enough." He says it softly, and it jars me more than if he'd matched my screaming. I've gone too far, crossed some line I should have seen but didn't.

"Sammy—"

"Take them!" Sammy throws the bottle at me. "Go ahead! Be my guest."

I lunge to catch it. My chest brushes the deer as I wrap my fingers around the cold glass of the bottle.

"That's it, Sammy!" I shout after him. "Walk away! You're too good for the rest of us!" But what I want to be shouting is that I didn't mean any of it. That I need him. That I want us to be close, like we used to be. That I'm sorry.

"Sammy!" I cry.

But he's faded into the fog. And I know he's not coming back.

There won't be a King of Second Chances, not tonight.

I sit by the deer on the roadside. My gaze darts from the doe to where Sammy disappeared, then to thousands of stars rising in eternal patterns.

"Sammy, come back!" I shout. But he's not there. He can't hear me.

I feel totally alone on an earth spinning out of control.

Wind rustles the leaves, and Sammy's words are still tangled there, whispering: *If God ever closes his eyes, then nobody sees me, and I'm not here.*

"I'm here," I whisper. "Don't close your eyes. Please don't close your eyes."

I can see the whole scene as if it's instant replay— me shouting at Sammy, scoring blow after blow. Why did I say those things to him? Was that really me screaming those hateful things? I don't want it to be me.

Dear God, I don't know who I am or what I'm doing anymore. If you really know me, then help me . . . because I can't do this anymore.

I look from the deer to the bottle in my fist. *But I can't make myself stop. And I'm tired. So tired.*

Shivering, still kneeling beside the lifeless doe, I listen. I don't hear God's voice coming from the stars. But I listen. And something inside me seems to open just wide enough to let in hope, hope that God hears my voice and recognizes it. And hope that I will hear and recognize his.

I don't know how long I stay there, kneeling by the side of the road, before headlights sweep over me and stay.

A car door opens, and footsteps pound the pavement behind me.

"Kyra?" Dad shouts. "Are you okay?" He kneels beside me. "You're shivering. Are you hurt? Where's Sammy?"

I make myself answer. "I killed the deer. Sammy's not hurt." But I know better.

Mom's heels click on the asphalt as she runs up. She's in her church clothes. Bethie's play. The play must be over. I close my eyes and try to see Bethany in her sheep's costume.

Mom fires questions at me, but I can't take them in. I'm shaking all over.

"Let's just get you home," Mom mutters, her arm around my shoulder, pulling me to my feet.

I don't fight any of it. Dad stays with the deer. Mom drives me home and puts me to bed the way she did when Sammy and I were little.

Sammy. He's gone when we get to the house.
I can't bear to think of him, but I can't stop the
thoughts.

Mom turns out my bedroom light and I lie there,
staring at the ceiling. Even now, even after everything that's happened, I think about taking one of
the pills in my purse and making it all go away, at
least for a while. But I don't take a pill.

I lie in the darkness and see the deer smashing
into my windshield. I try to think about God watching and knowing, and I turn my thoughts toward
God, hoping this is prayer, that I'm praying. And
after a while, for the first time in years, I fall asleep
talking to God.

■   ■   ■

The next morning, Sammy's already gone when
I wake up. I miss hearing the cartoon voices and
Sammy's laughter. I have to talk to him.

And I need help. *Sometimes everybody needs
a little help.*

But I don't go to my purse, to the glass bottle
and the orange pills. I don't know if I'll take one
in the next hour or even in the next minute. But
I don't take one right now. I don't throw them away
either. I'm not that strong.

I pray. I'm not even sure what I'm praying
because my mind wanders too much—to Sammy,
the deer, the play, the pills. But I do it anyway,
while I take my shower, while I brush my teeth,
while I get dressed.

■   ■   ■

"How are you feeling this morning, Kyra? Better?"
Mom asks when I come downstairs.

I nod.

She and Dad are dressed, and Dad holds out
Mom's sweater so she can slip into it. "Don't worry
about . . . well, about that thing last night," Dad
says. "It's all taken care of. Those things happen."

I nod again.

"You can drive your car," Dad continues. "I'll get
that dent fixed next week."

Mom smiles at me. "If you're sure you're okay,
we're off to shop for that new television. Great sales
today."

"Sure. I'm okay."

Dad has his hand on the doorknob. "Good! Call
us if you need us. I'll leave the cell on. Your mother
and I will be back in plenty of time to see our stars
onstage."

"We wouldn't miss that!" Mom assures me.
"Don't you worry."

Don't worry? I force a smile. "Great. See you
later then." I'm acting already. Last night it felt
like the world had changed, that I'd changed, too.
But here I am, same old actress, waving them off
as they exit stage right, shutting the door behind
them.

Only I don't want to act. That's a change. And
at least I've caught myself pretending. I saw it,
admitted it to myself. So maybe that's something.

Help me, God?

■ ■ ■

Sammy doesn't come home all afternoon. I've gone over and over in my head everything he said last night, everything I said, everything I'll say the minute he walks in.

But he doesn't walk in.

There's nothing in our house except me, the silence, and the pills in my purse that keep willing me to take one. I try to keep busy. I do my econ. I go over my lines.

Half a dozen times I start to call Dylan, then chicken out. Finally, I dial all the numbers and don't hang up.

"'Lo?"

"Hey, Bethie! You were dynamite last night!"

"Did you like it, Kyra?"

"Are you kidding? I loved it! And you said all your lines just right." I visualize Bethany in her costume and the little boy in shepherd robes. "Thanks, Bethie," I whisper, feeling like I could cry all over again.

Dylan's gone, working all day at his dad's lumberyard. Anyway, I don't know what I'd say to him. I can imagine what he thinks of me though.

I keep Bethany on the line, chatting with me until her mother calls her for supper.

Sammy's still not home. Every time I hear a car outside, I run to the window. I want to tell him I'm sorry, that I didn't mean any of the things I said, that I need him. I want to talk to him about God watching us.

■   ■   ■

When I can't wait any longer, I iron my costume
and drive myself to the gym to get ready for opening night. Dylan's car isn't in the school lot, and
neither is Sammy's. My peanut-butter sandwich, the
only thing I've eaten all day, sits in the pit of my
stomach. My head aches, and I know that the pills
in my purse could at least help with that. I pray,
but the war inside of me rages anyway. I can't take
my mind off the pills.

As soon as I step inside, Miranda comes running
up. "It's all set, Kyra! Everybody's coming to my
place after the play. I picked up chips and some
other junk. Ryan's bringing some stuff. Mitch is
coming."

"Have you seen Sammy, Miranda?"

"Huh? Not yet. He's coming to my party though.
At least he *said* he was coming."

"I really need to talk with him."

"I'll let him know, okay? But you better change
into your costume." Miranda nods toward the gown
I'm carrying. "Aren't you going to put your hair up
for Act 1?"

I go through the motions of getting ready. My
hands are trembling, and I need to calm down. My
neck is so stiff it hurts to pull the dress over my
head. I could take one pill, just one, or maybe a
second in the middle of the play so I wouldn't go
through what I did at dress rehearsal.

"You okay?" Miranda walks in with the hat
I have to change into between acts.

"Just a little edgy." Well, maybe a lot edgy. The gym is filling up. I hear them murmuring. My parents are probably out there. I can't remember a single line. *Sometimes everybody needs a little help.*

"Well, look," Miranda says, handing me a white envelope. "Somebody left this for you. I found it onstage, front and center."

I study the envelope. The only thing written on the outside is *Kyra,* printed in big letters on the front.

"Who's it from?" I ask, turning it over and untucking the flap.

"Like I'm into opening other people's mail? I don't know who." She sets the hat on our makeshift dressing table. "I've got to run. Mitch wants the props out."

Alone, I pull out the card. On the front is a cartoony picture of a lamb standing on his hind legs and holding a silver trophy over his head. I open the card and read:

> **Congratulations! We knew you could do it!**
> **From All of Us!**

At the bottom, it says: "Now I know in part; then I shall know fully, even as I am fully known. —1 Corinthians 13:12"

And it's signed: *Love, Dylan*

It's all I can do not to cry and wreck my makeup.

"Five minutes, people!" Mitch shouts.

I dash out onstage, looking frantically for Dylan.

When I spot him, standing by himself offstage, I run to him and hug him until neither of us can breathe. I don't let go, even when I hear the jokes shooting from all fronts:

"I wish *I* got to be Orlando!"

"What do you guys think this is? Romantic comedy?"

Finally, I let him go. "Dylan, there's so much I want to tell—"

"Now!" Mitch shouts.

"They'll be plenty of time," Dylan says. And I believe him.

We take our places. The curtain goes up. I watch, transfixed, as Dylan says the first lines of the play.

Sammy rushes onstage, and it's the first time I've seen him since the accident. He's solid and good, and I'm so proud of him I want to stop the show and hug him and apologize and promise to tell our parents the truth. But he exits left, the opposite side of the stage.

When I hear my cue, for a second I just stand there. I don't think I can go through with this.

"Go!" somebody behind me whispers and shoves me onto the stage.

As I make my entrance, my mouth feels like it's filled with sand. Words will have to pass through a desert to get out. I hear the audience shift in their seats. Legs cross. Arms fold. The spotlight sweeps the stage and comes to rest on me. A picture of the wide-eyed deer flashes through my mind. I want to run offstage, find Sammy, and turn back time.

"Kyra!" Mitch whispers loud, offstage.

I glance over at Dylan. His head is down, and I know he's praying.

I pray, too. *I need help, God. And you're it.*

I open my mouth, and the words come out. It's my voice. I'm too nervous to go for the British accent. But the lines are coming in the right places, and I start to go with them.

The scene moves forward. I have to be prompted once, and I garble a couple of lines, but I recover and keep going. And I'm not too bad and getting better by the end of Act 1.

■　　■　　■

After Act Two, Mitch takes me aside. "Kyra, you need to relax. Loosen up! Do whatever it takes, but get yourself loose." He squeezes my shoulder, then runs over to Miranda and whispers back and forth with her.

My hands shake, and I can't get my breath. I want so much to please Mitch. I don't want to let him down. It's not too late to take a pill. Just one. Just to get me through the rest of the performance.

"You're on!" Dylan strides up to me. "Break an ankle, kid."

I grin at him. It's like I can see all the way through him, down 10 layers to where Jesus lives inside of him. And I know it's what I want for my life too—to be known like that. By Dylan. And by Jesus.

I walk out onstage and plunge into my lines, the ones that lead to my scene with Miranda. When she comes onstage, I can feel the eyes of the audience shift to the tall brunette. They're watching her. She's good. I can't help comparing myself, my shaky performance to her solid one.

Then Dylan comes out, and we do the Act 3 scenes we've rehearsed together. The dialogue takes off. We snap our lines back and forth. His accent rubs off on me, and I hear myself sounding more and more British. We're grinning at each other, not just Orlando and Rosalind, but Dylan and Kyra. And I think it's an amazing thing that I'm enjoying this.

When the play ends and we take our bows, I know Shakespeare wouldn't have been pleased. I'm not kidding myself. We won't win the Tony. But we did it. We did all right. The applause is real, even if it is mostly from parents.

We take curtain calls, the whole cast, then five of us, until only Dylan and I are left onstage, holding hands and bowing. But I know that deep inside, as he squeezes my hand, we're not just bowing to the audience.

God is watching.

As soon as the curtain closes for the final time, Dylan turns to me. "Kyra, come fishing with me tonight."

Without a moment's hesitation or a second thought, I answer, "Yes!" I don't care where we're going or what anybody thinks about it. "Give me a minute to find Sammy. Then I'm all yours."

I look onstage, offstage, and in the gym. Sammy isn't anywhere.

"Sammy took off before the last curtain call," Brent says.

I can't stand not making things right with Sammy. But it will have to wait.

"Are you ready, Kyra?" Miranda juggles the bags and costumes in her arms. "Need a ride?"

"I'm not coming, Miranda."

She drops her bag of shoes. "You've got to be kidding! Everybody's going to be there! You can't pull a no-show!"

"Thanks anyway. I'll call you tomorrow. Tonight I've got a date with a fish."

28

Dylan drives us to McCray's farm, and we walk across the pasture and down the little hill to our silver chariot. The rowboat's right where we left it that awful night when I got drunk with Tyrone. I don't want to think about it, but I let myself think anyway because I don't ever want to feel like that, act like that, again.

We push the boat to the edge of the pond, jump in, and shove off. Water splashes the tinny sides of the boat. Crickets are warming up at the shore, singing in their own language. We don't need flashlights. The moon hangs low, streaking the water sparkly white. Overhanging trees poke out buds. I can smell corn from somewhere, grass, and maybe fish.

Dylan rows out, stopping on the moonlight carpet

in the middle of the pond. The wind rustles the leaves and ripples the water. The only thing that could make this moment better would be to know Sammy forgives me.

"What is it?" Dylan asks.

I start to tell him that it's nothing. I don't want to spoil this night. But I'm so tired of lying and pretending. "It's Sammy." And I tell Dylan everything—about Mom's pills, how I let them think it was Sammy, our horrible fight after I hit the deer. "I need to tell Sammy how sorry I am. And tell my parents the truth."

Dylan moves to my side of the boat and puts his arm around me. "Then that's what you'll do."

"Can't I just stay here forever, Dylan?"

He laughs. "Sounds good to me."

"It's not going to be easy, is it? I'll tell my parents or go back to school, and all that stress is going to come right back."

He paddles so we can face the moon. "The stress isn't going anywhere, Kyra . . . but neither is God."

Dylan sticks plastic worms on our hooks, and we cast our lines out. We talk and fish, as the moon rises higher and higher. We talk about college and what we want to do afterwards. I catch two fish, and he catches one, and we throw them all back in. And when we're not talking, I don't feel like I have to make up conversation. It's okay this way.

"So," Dylan says, casting his line behind us, "if your house burned down, Kyra James, what three things would you take with you?"

I don't have to stop and think. Most of the times

when I've played this game with other people,
I answered the way I thought they'd want me to
answer. For my parents, I'd list the most recent gifts
they'd given me. With girlfriends, I'd name lipstick,
favorite shoes, things like that. With guys, I'd
answer according to what *they* liked.

Not now. "Jesus. And you, Dylan. And Sammy."

We fish some more. Dylan's as wonderful as ever,
but my mood shifts. I can't stop thinking about
Sammy.

"What's up?" Dylan asks.

I smile at him. "Guess you know me past Layer
One again, huh? It's Sammy. I'm not going to be all
right until I can talk to him."

"Want to go find him?"

"You mean it?" I study Dylan—his strong chin,
his high cheekbones, his eyes. It's a face that hides
nothing. "Thanks, Dylan."

He takes the oars and swings the boat around
toward the shore. My purse falls to the floor.

"Dylan, wait!" I pick up my purse. "There's something I have to do first." I take out the tiny glass
bottle, unscrew the lid. Then holding it over the side
of the boat, I empty it. The small orange dots *plink*
into the pond. The water stirs around them, over-
powers them, breaks them down until they disappear
in the ripples, washed away with sticks and leaves.

Dylan doesn't say a word.

I breathe in the scent of the pond water, Dylan's
clean-soap smell, spring grasses at the water's edge.
And I get another idea. I rinse the bottle, get it as
dry as I can. Then I wave it above my head and

capture the smell of the pond, the fish, the moon-light, spring on the branches, and this moment. "This is for Bethie."

"Robin Hood strikes again," Dylan says. He leans over, puts his hand around the back of my neck, and gently kisses me.

A horn honks.

We laugh and sit back up straight. It honks again.

Dylan rows to shore as Jamal stumbles down the hill, waving his arms and shouting.

"What is it?" Dylan shouts back. He pulls the boat to shore and climbs out.

"I've been looking all over for you guys. Bethany's the one who told me you'd be out here. I almost didn't even try it."

I get out of the boat, thinking Miranda has sent reinforcements to get us to her party.

"What's going on, Jamal?" Dylan isn't joking. Something's in his voice.

Already I feel icy fingers grab the pit of my stomach. I know before Jamal answers.

"It's Sammy, man."

"What's wrong with Sammy?" My voice is hoarse and wavering.

Jamal keeps running his hand over his head. "We were all at Miranda's, partying. Nothing special. Then Sammy came in. We gave him a hard time. You know, last-minute party boy, that jazz. So he's having a beer or maybe a couple, like the rest of us."

I want to shake him, make him talk faster. "Then *what?*"

"Then . . . I don't know. He's just not acting like Sammy. It's weird." Jamal looks right at me. "I think you ought to come."

■ ■ ■

Jamal's car is closest, so I jump in with him. Dylan follows us. My heart races so fast it hurts. I'm scared, terrified. The deer flashes into my mind, sprawled lifeless on the road.

Something has happened to Sammy. I feel it inside me, carried in the blood that courses through my veins and makes my heart pound.

"Can't you drive any faster, Jamal?"

I want him to laugh, to tell me I'm getting all worked up over nothing. But he doesn't. He grips the steering wheel and floors it.

As soon as we turn onto Miranda's street, I hear the party. Even in the car, I feel the pulsating beats of the music. Cars litter the lawn, parked in every direction as if someone has shaken them in his fist and tossed them down like pick-up sticks or jelly beans.

"Let me out!" I scream, already opening the door before Jamal can come to a stop. I stumble out and take off running, weaving through cars, shoving past people on the walk, pushing through the crowd on the step, and then forcing my way upstairs to the apartment. The door's wide open.

"Kyra!"

"Hey! You made it!"

I ignore everybody, everything. "Sammy! Sammy? Where are you?"

Tressa comes up and offers me her beer. "Well, it's about ti—"

"Where is he? Where's my brother?"

"Sammy?"

I want to smack her. "Tressa! Where's Sammy?"

Frowning, she shrugs. "I don't know. He was around here earlier." She breaks into a big grin. "You should have seen him. He was *so* funny!"

I shove her out of my way and into Hale Ramsey, who almost falls backwards. I keep pressing through the front room until I see Tyrone sitting by himself in the easy chair. I stop in front of him and yell, "Where's Sammy?"

Tyrone shakes his head. Something in his eyes makes me shiver.

"Tyrone, I'm not kidding. Where is—?"

He tilts his head toward the far end of the room.

I make my way through, passing Brianna, who's arguing with somebody. Someone's shouting for a joint. People blur past me. Sounds mesh together into a steady roar.

"Hey, Kyra! You came! I knew you wouldn't miss this." Miranda starts toward me, trips, then gets her balance. "Mitch was—"

"Where's Sammy?" I shout, pushing between two jocks to get to her. She smells like beer, and her eyes are murky.

"Over there." She nods toward the couch. "He's had a *great* time."

Turning my back on her, I race to the old purple couch. The first thing I recognize is Sammy's sneaker, lopped over the arm of the sofa. Then I see

Sammy, stretched out, lying on his back, his arm
dangling over the side.

I run to him and kneel beside the couch. "Sammy?
Sammy!" I pick up his hand, and it feels too cold.
When I let it go, it drops limp.

"What's the matter with him? What's wrong
with Sammy?" I scream, glancing around for help.
"Miranda?"

"He's asleep." Miranda sounds asleep herself.
"Wanna drink?"

"He is *not* asleep, Miranda!" I wheel back around
to look at my brother. He isn't moving. His face is
pale and empty, as if nothing is inside of him. With
the back of my hand I feel his forehead. Then I
touch his cheeks. "Wake up! Sammy! Wake up!" I'm
touching his cheeks, harder and harder, until I hear
the slap of my palms on his face.

"Easy, girl," Miranda coos. "He just had a little
too much to drink is all."

But I'm not listening to her. Not to anybody.
Voices are telling me to calm down. I hear Jamal
calling for Sammy. Dylan's voice carries through the
crowd. He's yelling for me, for Sammy.

"Something's wrong!" I cry to Dylan or to God.
I grab Sammy's shoulders and shake him. "You
have to wake up! Sammy, I'm sorry. I didn't mean–
I don't–please! I need you!"

I feel an arm on my shoulder, and I jump.

"Hey . . . Kyra?" Miranda looks scared now, but
not for Sammy. For me. "Just chill."

"Call 911!"

Miranda backs up. "Just a minute, Kyra."

"Where's the phone?"

"Okay. I'll be right back." She staggers off toward the kitchen.

I see Dylan talking to Tyrone across the room. "Dylan!"

He races toward me.

"Sammy's not waking up!" I shout it, but Dylan shakes his head like he can't hear me. Somebody pushes in front of him, and I can't see Dylan anymore.

Miranda comes back from the kitchen. "Let's get him some coffee."

A crowd has gathered around the sofa now. "Just get him in the shower!" someone suggests. I think it's Manny, but my eyes are blurry with tears. Can't they see what I see?

Frantic, I turn on Miranda. She's not carrying the phone. "Did you call?" She doesn't answer. "Where's the phone, Miranda?"

She still doesn't answer.

I jump to my feet and lunge at her, grabbing her arm and not letting go. "Call 911 *right now!* I'm not kidding!"

Dylan comes beside me and puts his arm around me.

Miranda pries my fingers from her arm and backs away. "Okay!" She heads back to the kitchen.

I look up at Dylan. "Something's really wrong with Sammy, Dylan." I choke on the words and have to gasp to get my breath.

"Are you all right?" Dylan asks, pounding my back until I stop choking. Then he goes over to

Sammy. Dylan lifts Sammy's eyelid. He puts his ear
to my brother's chest. Frowning, he turns to me.
"See if Miranda got through to emergency."

I charge into the kitchen. "Miranda!"

She's standing over the sink, staring at the drain.

"Where is it?" I scream. "Where's the freaking
phone?"

She glances around the kitchen as if she doesn't
know where *she* is, much less where the phone is.
"I dunno."

I start to ask again. Then I remember. There's
another phone in this house.

Running down the hall to Shelby's room, my
heart is praying, even though I can't form words.
I throw open the door and spot the blue phone next
to the bed. It takes me two tries to get the numbers
right.

"911. Is this—"

"Help! My brother! Something's wrong with him!
I think—you have to come! Now! He won't wake up!"

"I need you to calm down, ma'am. Where—?"

"Calm down?" My hand is shaking so hard, the
phone slips. I catch it and scream at the idiot who
still isn't sending help. "Now! You have to come
right now!"

"Give us the address." Her voice is calm, even.
Like a machine. "I need your name and the address.
Do you understand?"

"Kyra James! But I'm not home. I'm—" The breath
goes out of me. I can't remember the address. The
street name. Anything. I glance around, panic roaring in my ears so I can't hear the woman.

Dylan's standing in the doorway. He reaches out, and I give him the phone.

He takes over, giving the address, names, thanking them. When he hangs up, he takes my arm and pulls me out of the room and back to Sammy.

The house is almost quiet now. A door slams. Jamal's the only one still there. And Miranda. She's holding Sammy's hand and crying. Somebody's covered my brother with a red blanket. I want to throw it off. I want Sammy to throw it off, to get up, to laugh and say, "Gotcha!"

But he doesn't.

We wait. But I can't stand it. Sammy doesn't move. Miranda won't leave. I don't want her near my brother.

"Why aren't they here yet?" And just as I say it, I hear the siren. I'm not thinking, but my legs are moving and running, out the door, down the stairs. I don't want them to miss the apartment.

Red lights flash and spin. Sirens get louder, then swallow themselves.

"Here!" I shout as loud as I can. "He's in here! Hurry!"

Two paramedics run up the sidewalk. They're carrying a stretcher. A stretcher for Sammy.

"Hurry! Up the stairs! One more flight!"

We thunder up the steps and into the apartment. I let them run past me to Sammy. Creeping to the couch, I see them tear open Sammy's shirt. Dylan comes and puts his arm around me. We watch.

It can't be happening. Not to Sammy.

One of the paramedics pulls out a cell or a walkie-talkie and talks into it. I hear " . . . possible drug overdose. No blood pressure. We're bringing him in. . . . Right. Possible cardiac arrest."

My knees buckle, and Dylan's arm tightens around my waist.

The paramedic looks up at us. "What did he take?"

I can't speak. Sammy? What did *he* take? But he wouldn't. Except in my head I hear myself yelling at him, shouting at my brother that he *should* take drugs, that he needed to be more fun . . . and I know whatever's happening to him is my fault.

"I don't know what he might have had," Dylan answers. He turns to Miranda. "Miranda?"

She doesn't move, doesn't answer.

"I need to know if he's allergic to anything." The paramedic is pleading with us to know something, anything.

I shake my head.

Two policemen storm the apartment. They talk with the paramedics, but the medics are already lifting Sammy onto the stretcher.

"I'm going with him!" I cry.

The cop looks at me. Dylan says something to them. Then they turn to Miranda.

Dylan and I run after the paramedics and follow them as they carry Sammy down the stairs and out to the ambulance.

■ ■ ■

At the hospital, they try. They push tubes into Sammy, pound on his heart, and try to pump life back into him.

But they can't. They don't. They are too late. We all are.

Epilogue

It's been two months since the night at Miranda's house. And every day has been long, filled with guilt. A litany of *what ifs* still plays in my head—what if I hadn't shouted hateful things at Sammy the last time I saw him? What if he hadn't found the bottle of pills in my purse? What if I'd never taken the first pill?

I finished our senior year somehow, but most days I yearned for pills to help me through it. Once, on the one-week anniversary of Sammy's murder, our birthday, I went to the medicine cabinet and probably would have taken at least two of Mom's pills, but she'd moved them. I'd told my parents everything by then.

That was hard. At first they didn't even believe their little Kyra could have done the things I did. But they believe me now. I'm off the pedestal. Things aren't smooth at home, but we're talking more, really talking. And we're all learning a lot about forgiveness.

It hasn't been easy diving down past Layers One and Two. Lots of junk down there. Lots of guilt. Sometimes I think I'd be better off not knowing. Then I look at the plaque Dylan gave me on my birthday. Sammy's birthday. It's from a Psalm: *But you desire honesty from the heart, so you can teach me to be wise in my inmost being.* I want to be wise, so I'm trying not to lie to myself. I know where that got me, where it got all of us.

Dylan says God loves me, "zits and all," which is so Dylan. He's been great, less than a phone call away. But we both make sure I'm leaning on Christ, not Dylan. And it's made us steadier, deeper.

I've gone over and over why Sammy died and not me. *He* was supposed to be the twin of second chances. But he didn't get a second chance. One time, one bad choice. And he's dead. It should have been me, all the chances I took, all the things I did that were wrong. Wrong. In so many ways. I guess I'll never understand that part.

I miss Sammy every day. All day. I have to live with the memory of those horrible things I said to him. Even now, some nights I wake up in a cold sweat, and I say out loud all the things I wish I could have said to Sammy, how sorry I am, how I'd do anything, *anything*, to take it back.

Now I'm 18, and my twin will always be 17. The gap will get wider and wider. And a part of me will stay back there with him, a carved-out piece I won't ever get back.

In the halls at school I'll see a shock of hair or a shirt like Sammy's, and I want to run after the guy. Then it hits me. Sammy is dead.

I even miss Miranda. Lots of things have come out about Miranda. Turns out she was a better actress than all of us. A lot of things have come out about a lot of people—Tyrone, Hale . . . Mitch. I suppose things will keep coming out, especially at the trial.

And Sammy. I had no idea how much Miranda meant to him, not until I found a drawerful of poems he'd written. Poems. Who knew? And the best poems were about "Randi."

God's working on me to forgive Miranda, to forgive Tyrone, and to forgive myself. Maybe someday I'll get to Mitchell Wade.

■   ■   ■

The doors to the courtroom finally burst open, and the prosecutor strides out and straight to my bench. Dylan's close behind her. I walk over to meet them.

"How did it go, Dylan?" I ask.

He takes my hand and squeezes it. "Fine. And you'll do fine, too."

"It's time, Kyra." The prosecutor straightens his maroon-striped tie. "Your turn."

My turn. It *is* my turn. My time. And no matter what happens in that courtroom, I promise to tell the truth, the whole truth, and nothing but the truth.

So help me, God.

degrees OF GUILT

Sammy's dead . . . they each played a part.
Kyra, his twin sister. Miranda, the girl
he loved. And Tyrone, a friend from school.

WHAT'S THE REAL STORY?

There's always more than
one point of view—read all three.

kyra's story
DANDI DALEY MACKALL

miranda's story
MELODY CARLSON

tyrone's story
SIGMUND BROUWER

For insider info and surprising revelations, go to
www.degreesofguilt.com.
Enter code guilt01 and you'll be able to watch Kyra's
video interview and read her court transcript too.

A Sneak Peek at Miranda's Story . . .

It's 10 minutes before fifth period when I get
to school, and the halls are fairly vacant because
kids are still at lunch. As I walk to my AP history
class, it occurs to me that I could drop this class and
still graduate. In fact, I could easily drop three
classes and graduate. I only took these AP classes
because Ms. Whitman said it would increase my
chances of getting into a good college, possibly even
on a scholarship. Funny how that used to be terribly
important.

No one is in the classroom yet, and instead of
finding a front seat, I go for the back row, far corner, next to the window. I open my history book
and pretend to be reading, but my eyes don't focus
on the page. I remember how I used to do this on a
regular basis back in middle school—pretend to be

invisible—and it usually worked. No one ever wanted to sit next to me or converse or even look at me back when I was a nobody. I want to be a nobody again. It shouldn't be that hard.

Kids are coming in now. I feel them looking at me, and I hear their whispers. I try not to imagine what they're saying, thinking. But I can't help myself. "There's the girl who killed Sammy James." Or "Can you believe she has the guts to show her face here, after what she did?" Or "Poor Kyra . . . she used to think Miranda was her friend."

I turn and look out the window, out across the back field where Taylor and Rebecca and I used to jog together for soccer practice, laughing and joking, back when I was human. Dylan is in this class. I hear him greeting Jamie, a boyfriend I once had— back in another lifetime. I can feel the two of them scrutinizing me as they find their seats. They are both too nice to say anything mean, but I can guess what they're thinking. They were both close to Sammy. Even though they go to church and claim to be good Christians, I'm certain they must both hate me. How could they not? *I* hate me.

A Sneak Peek at Tyrone's Story . . .

Macon, Iowa, is a small town. The kind of town where farmers actually drive tractors to the post office and the women trade recipes down at the local grocery store. I did not grow up here, of course. I grew up in Chicago, in an area of luxury high-rises that overlooked Lake Michigan.

It wasn't until my freshman year that I arrived in Macon, straight from a private school in Chicago where we all wore identical school uniforms and demerits were issued for shirts, ties, or pants that weren't sufficiently ironed free of any wrinkles. No wonder, huh, that I've decided to wear what I like when I like, even if that means turning shirts inside out to hide the corporate labels.

Any new school is tough to crack. It's tough enough to go from an elite private school to a rowdy public school. But imagine what it's like on the first day when basically all the other students have known each other their entire lives.

Because that was Macon High. Small, filled with classes where all the students had been in the same classes together since their kindergarten years.

It took me six months to find my niche, to stake it out, and to protect it so that at least I was accepted as part of the scenery. Not that I fit in. But I was accepted for not fitting in.

I wasn't alone in feeling like a stranger on that first day. There was one other person new to the school.

Hale Ramsey.

Who would immediately share my misery.

And, I was to find out later, much much more.

About the Author

Dandi Daley Mackall has published 330 books for
children, teens, and adults, with sales of three and
a half million in 22 countries. In addition to *Kyra's
Story*, her young adult fiction best-sellers include
six titles in the new Winnie the Horse Gentler series
(Tyndale), including *Wild Thing, Eager Star, Bold
Beauty, Midnight Mystery, Unhappy Appy*, and
Gift Horse. She's also written three nonfiction books
for high school students on having success in the
workplace: *Problem Solving, Teamwork*, and *Self-
Development* (Ferguson).

Currently Dandi conducts writing assemblies
and workshops across the U.S. She writes from
rural Ohio, where she lives with her husband, Joe,
and three children—Jen, Katy, and Dan—as well as
two horses, a dog, a cat, and two newts. You can
visit Dandi at www.dandibooks.com.

www.areUthirsty.com
www.degreesofguilt.com